Millennium Spies

Louise Dale

Dragonheart
Publishing

Published in Great Britain in 2004
Dragonheart Publishing, The Grey House, Main Street,
Carlton-on-Trent, Newark, Nottinghamshire NG23 6NW

www.dragonheartpublishing.co.uk

British Cataloguing in Publication Data.
A catalogue record of this book is available from the British
Library

ISBN 0 9543773 2 X

Cover painting by Ian R. Ward, Mansfield, Nottinghamshire
Map and Family Tree by Thurbans, Surrey

The Time Trigger Series:
    The Curse of Rocamadour
    The Keys of Rome
    Millennium Spies
    American Pilgrims (Provisional title - for autumn 2004)

Typesetting and production by
Richard Joseph Publishers Ltd, PO Box 15, Devon EX38 8ZJ

Printed in Great Britain by Creative Print & Design Group,
Middlesex UB7 0LW

For Charlotte

Contents

England at the turn of the first millennium

Family Tree: the relationships of the historical characters in *Millennium Spies*

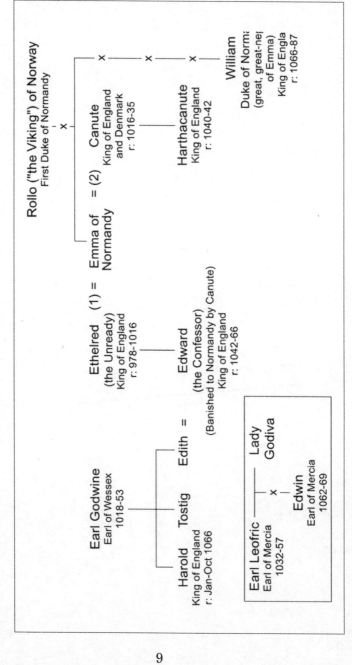

Rollo ("the Viking") of Norway
First Duke of Normandy

Ethelred (1) = Emma of = (2) Canute
(the Unready)   Normandy   King of England
King of England   and Denmark
r: 978-1016   r: 1016-35

Edward   Harthacanute
(the Confessor)   King of England
(Banished to Normandy by Canute)   r: 1040-42
King of England
r: 1042-66

William
Duke of Norm:
(great, great-ne|
of Emma)
King of Engla
r: 1066-87

Earl Godwine
Earl of Wessex
1018-53

Edith =

Harold   Tostig
King of England
r: Jan-Oct 1066

Earl Leofric ——— Lady
Earl of Mercia   Godiva
1032-57
                Edwin
                Earl of Mercia
                1062-69

1

Dark Age

Viking blood and guts had long since lost their charm. Alice was starting to feel drowsy. She propped herself up on one arm and closed her eyes to doze, trying to look as if she was still listening to the teacher. Mr Picket's swaying movements in front of the blackboard were hypnotic. Robert was happy though. He was so absorbed, his mouth was open. Alice nudged him.

"You'll catch a fly," she said.

Robert clamped his jaw shut.

"*...Saxon bodies bridged the moor like a stepping-stone causeway for the frenzied warriors.*" Mr Picket swayed and closed the history book just as the bell rang. "For homework this weekend, I'd like you all to write an essay on how the battle of Stamford Bridge changed English history."

"Another essay!" groaned Robert. "If I don't finish my French this weekend, I'll get detention."

"I'll do yours for a fiver," offered Alice, packing away her things.

"No way! I need that money for my new phone card," said Robert. "Anyway, I thought you were going somewhere this weekend?"

"I am, but only to my nan's. There won't be much to do, except take Keeper for walks," said Alice.

"Keeper?" said Robert.

"Nan's dog. He's a black, Flat-coated Retriever. I take him for long walks on the beach or up to the windmill."

"That sounds cool. Wish I was going," said Robert.

They wandered down the stairs. "I'm going to put some gory bits in my essay this time. I liked the bit when one of them got shot in the throat with an arrow."

Alice wrinkled up her nose in disgust.

"I think I'm going to include a bit about King Harold's traitor brother," she said.

"Old Toastie?" said Robert.

"Yes. Tostig. It is a great name isn't it?" said Alice. "Wouldn't fancy bumping into him in the dark, though. He sounds really nasty." At the doorway of the humanities block, they waited as a crowd of older girls barged through. "I wonder why he didn't agree to his brother's offer of forgiveness? He must have known he'd die if he stayed and fought. Harold's army was obviously going to beat the Viking invaders."

"Surrender wouldn't have been cool back then," said Robert. "You were in it to the death. Tostig's Viking friends would have killed him with an arrow in the back. He was doomed either way."

Sarah ran across the playground towards them.

"Hi!" said Alice. "How was cookery, then? What's in the basket?"

Robert started poking at the tea towel cover.

"Oy! Fingers off!" said Sarah.

"Gotta go," said Robert. "Text me," he added, as he ran off towards a group of boys from their year.

Alice felt herself blushing before Sarah even spoke.

"Ooh! Texting each other are we?" said Sarah.

"It's not what you think," said Alice. "We're just friends."

Sarah gave Alice a look of fake disbelief. Alice shrugged, heaved her rucksack onto her back and started to walk away.

"O.K," said Sarah, running after her. "I know.

You're just friends. Listen... do you fancy going to see the new James Bond film tomorrow?"

"Can't," said Alice. "Mum's going to London to some conference. My sister's going to have a sleepover at her friends and I'm going to my grandmother's in Essex. Maybe next weekend?"

Sarah frowned and nodded.

"Come on!" said Alice. "Let's get an iced bun on the way to the bus stop."

The baker's shop was half way between the school and Alice's bus stop. In the mornings, the iced buns were really fresh and soft. The pink icing was still sticky and it dripped down the sides of the warm dough. Tonight, the iced buns were sold out, but there were two chocolate éclairs at the side of the cabinet.

"Umm," muttered Alice. "But I haven't got enough money for one of those."

"I have," said Sarah. "If I have a flapjack."

"Are you sure?" said Alice.

"Course. You can buy me something next week."

"Cheers," said Alice. She punched her friend amicably on the arm.

They waited at the bus stop in silence. It was impossible to talk while wrestling with a chocolate éclair. Alice's bus came first. Having swallowed her mouthful, she mimed 'see you next week' to Sarah through the window, before settling back for the journey home. She daydreamed all the way home, about violent Dark Age battles and Viking longships.

That night, she dreamt too. Her dreams were almost real. A Viking king was trying to find her. He needed her help. Alice was running from some kind of treachery. She desperately needed to find a Time Trigger to escape.

The next morning, she was woken up when her mum opened the curtains. That always annoyed Alice. She turned over in bed.

"Alice, love..."

Her mum sat down on the bed.

"It's too early," groaned Alice from under the edge of her duvet. "It's Saturday!"

"I know, love. But we've got to leave soon. And the plans have changed slightly. Felicity Davenport has just telephoned."

Alice's eyes shot open.

"Robert's mum?"

"Yes. His father has had an accident. Nothing too serious, but he's in hospital and Mrs Davenport wondered if Robert could stay with you at Aunty Jane's tonight."

Alice sat up.

"Did you say yes?" she asked.

"I rang Aunty Jane."

"And..."

"She said fine. You'll have to sleep on a camp bed in Nan's room though. Aunty Jane and Uncle Jim have only got one other room since Nan came to live with them, and Robert will have to have that."

A huge grin spread across Alice's face. It was O.K. at the house in Essex, but once her aunt and uncle had gone to work it was a bit quiet. The highlights of staying there were walking Keeper the dog and playing cards with Nan. But now she'd have a friend. She could show Robert her secret place up by the windmill. Then she had an even more exciting thought. What if they found a Time Trigger again? It would need to be something connected with the past that would trigger their powers to time travel on a quest. They might have another adventure! They had a knack of doing that whenever they went somewhere unusual together.

She jumped out of bed with uncharacteristic speed and started shoving clothes and other essentials into her sports grip.

"Didn't you do all that last night like I asked you?" said her mother, looking over her shoulder.

"Oops! Sorry! Got carried away reading the last few chapters of my book," said Alice.

"Well, get a move on!" said her mum. "Mrs Davenport will be here with Robert in ten minutes, and time and tide won't wait for any man!"

Alice Hemstock, the time traveller, smiled to herself as she pulled on her jeans and T-shirt.

"Actually," she muttered when her mum was out of sight, "... time does wait for me sometimes."

2

Time Tunnel

Alice looked around her room and remembered her floppy dog, bald in places from a thousand cuddles. She heard her mum shout at her to come down, for the third time.

Robert was in the kitchen. He grinned, pointing at her hair.

"Oh, no!" said Alice, clamping her hands on her head. "I haven't brushed my hair!"

"Alice!" said her mum, clearly annoyed. "There's no time..."

"Hello, Mrs Davenport," said Alice. Before her mum could protest, which she was unlikely to do too loudly in front of visitors, Alice dived into the downstairs toilet to brush her strawberry blond hair and smooth it into a bobble. She heard Mrs Davenport's car leaving.

"Really sorry!" she said, smiling hopefully at her mum as she ran out to the car.

The journey to the house in Essex took a couple of hours from Newark. Alice hoped they would be there in time for a late cooked breakfast. Nan usually made great bacon rolls.

It was a warm day for June. Alice's aunt and uncle lived at the bottom of a country lane. Alice saw her nan lying along the swinging garden seat as soon as they rounded the corner into the driveway. Nan was fast asleep under the fringed canopy with her mouth open, the seat rocking gently in the breeze. Robert raised his eyebrows mischievously. But before he could do anything, Alice's grandmother sat up, woken by the loud barking behind the garden gate.

"Hi, Nan!" called Alice, slamming the car door shut.

She ran over and gave her grandmother a huge hug.

"And this young man must be Robert," said Nan with a soft Scottish accent.

"Hello Mrs...Mrs..." Robert looked at Alice for help.

"Och! Just call me Nan!" said Alice's grandmother.

After a brief chat with Nan and a kiss for Alice, Mrs Hemstock rushed off to her meeting.

"I think we'd better introduce you to Keeper, young Robert," said Nan, nodding in the direction of the barking. "You two could take him for a wee walk while I put some bacon on. What do you think?"

"Umm. Yes please Nan!" said Alice. She put her arms around her grandmother's stout frame. Then she noticed Robert's frown. "Oh, don't worry about Keeper. He's a softy!"

"Big softy, by the sounds of it," said Robert.

Alice's grandmother stood on tiptoe and lifted the latch on the other side of the gate. Before she had opened it much more than a chink, a wet, black nose appeared and the gate flew open. An inky shape rocketed through the opening. It was as much as Alice could do to stay standing. She tickled and tugged at the shiny fur, and pushed the dog's head away when she was wet from his licking.

"Down! Keeper...down!" she yelled.

Keeper obeyed, but then immediately repeated the whole process with Robert.

"I think he likes you," said Nan, laughing. "Here's his lead. Take him down the lane a bit."

Alice clipped the lead onto Keeper's collar.

"Calm down, boy," she said. "I know... I

17

know ... we ARE going for a walk."

Keeper almost dragged Alice down the drive.

"We'll put our stuff inside when we come back," yelled Robert as they side stepped around their bags.

"Come on," said Alice. "I want to show you something."

Keeper led Alice and Robert down the lane. The countryside hummed in the early summer heat. After about half a mile, Alice took a footpath over a stile and across some fields. When they reached the summit of a gentle hill, they stopped.

"Wow!" said Robert.

Alice grinned. This was one of her favourite places in the whole world and one of the best views she knew. Only a few metres away stood a derelict windmill, its torn sails creaking in the breeze. And beyond it was the sea.

"I've always loved this place," said Alice. "It feels good here. I sit with my back against the old windmill and think and talk to Keeper."

Robert looked at Alice for a moment. His eyes smiled with admiration.

"He must know all your secrets then," he said.

"Maybe. He certainly got me good marks in one of my English stories last term. I wrote about him and this place when we had to discuss our best friend."

"And I thought you'd have written about me," said Robert.

Alice scoffed.

"You can see the River Crouch on that side and across Foulness Island to the sea that way," she said.

"What was that noise?" said Robert suddenly.

Keeper growled at the windmill. Another crackle came from behind it.

Alice started to feel nervous.

"Rob, if there's someone there, let's go," she said.

18

"Hello! Anyone there?" called Robert.

Alice looked down at Keeper, but he'd relaxed again.

"Nobody's here. Just us," said Robert. "I'm going to explore."

He disappeared round one side of the shadowy structure. Wisps of cloud graced the blue sky and the only sounds came from birds and insects going about their business.

Then she heard it again. So did Keeper. This time, he barked. Alice stood very still. She could feel Keeper's body tensing and straining, but she kept the lead short. Then she saw something that made her heart leap.

A man was backing out from the other side of the windmill. He had a beard and long, flaxen hair and was strangely dressed in a cloak and tunic, with garters tied like thick laces criss-crossing around his muscular calves above leather boots. An axe and dagger hung from his belt. He saw Alice and Keeper and stopped. Slowly, he loosened his buckle. The belt and weapons clattered to the ground.

"I mean you no harm," said the man. "I come as a fellow traveller in need of help. Please..." He looked at Keeper. "Please, tell your animal to stand down. I am a friend."

Robert slipped across to Alice.

"He was spying on us," said Robert. "Don't trust him."

"Don't worry, I don't," said Alice. "Take a few steps back, then run! I'll let Keeper off his lead."

"Please...wait! You are Alice and Robert of Mercia, are you not? You are time travellers in this universe like me. I have made many perilous journeys here, trying to find you. I need your help in a matter of the greatest urgency to our kingdom."

Alice frowned at him.

"You don't believe him, do you?" whispered Robert.

"Prove it!" said Alice.

Robert looked at her in surprise.

"He knows about us. He might be telling the truth," said Alice.

"Look closely about me, my friends," said the man. "Do you see the walls of power?"

"No," said Alice.

"Wait a minute," said Robert. "Look out to sea, Alice. The view ... it's gone all shimmery."

"Oh, yes," said Alice.

She squinted and began to see something. In a circle extending behind the man was a ring of flickering air that distorted the views beyond like a heat haze. It extended upwards as far as she could see.

"O.K.," said Robert. "What is it?"

"It is a Time Tunnel," said the man. "I used a Time Trigger to create it. It has protected me when I travelled forwards to reach you. Travelling forwards in time can be very dangerous, as you know, but I have come to you as the prophecy in the runes directed. You are also two of the chosen ones who have the power to time travel. You have already learned well how to harness the power of time by holding a Time Trigger and concentrating on where you wish to be. When you are older and wiser in the lore of time travel, you too, may learn to open Time Tunnels. I have even heard of some whose powers are so great that they no longer need a Time Trigger to travel. But enough of that. I do not have long before I must return."

"And you are ... " said Robert.

"I am Canute, King of England and Denmark," said the man. "And I need your help."

3

The Amber Marbles

Robert raised one eyebrow, in the way he did when he was surprised.

"Why don't we all sit and talk like civilized human beings," said the king.

Alice looked across at Robert. He shrugged. Slowly, they both sat down. Alice crouched on one knee so that she could get up quickly if she needed to. Keeper flopped onto the grass beside her.

"I have heard of you," said Alice. "The village of Canewdon over there is named after King Canute."

"Yes," said the king, with a smile. "I saw that on one of my previous journeys."

"You have been here before?" said Alice.

"Oh, I have travelled here several times to look for you. The runes said in one millennium."

"How did you know we would come here?" said Robert.

"It is written on the ancient runestones that you would. In fact, I came one time when you were alone with your dog, Alice. I realised it was not the right time because Robert was not with you, so I did not reveal myself."

"You mean you've been spying on me?" said Alice in alarm.

"Yes. Time travellers do. You should know that. Invisible spies on secret missions."

Robert smiled.

"We have been able to watch people," he said. "But only when we have travelled backwards in time. You have travelled forwards. I thought that after doing that a few times, it would imprison the traveller in the future."

"Yes, it would if the travel was done recklessly, just for the sake of it, using a Time Trigger. But you are safe if you travel forwards with a Trigger as the direct requirement of a quest. And you are always safe if you have the power to create a Time Tunnel."

"O...K..." said Robert. "So that means that either you are on a time travelling quest of your own, or...because you used a Time Tunnel, maybe you're not?"

For a moment, a flicker of annoyance flashed across the man's dangerous eyes. His body stiffened.

"Of course I am on a quest. I have been guided by the runestones. I opened this tunnel as well, just to be on the safe side."

Alice felt the seeds of fear growing inside her. There was something she did not trust about Canute.

"Right," said Robert. "Well...putting aside the Time Tunnel issue for a minute, what's your quest?"

"I will speak plainly," said Canute. "I am here to give you something. It is written in the ancient runestones that two young travellers would be at this place just after the turn of the next millennium, in the year that the moon blacks out the sun."

"The moon blacks out the sun? Do you mean an eclipse?" said Robert.

King Canute nodded.

"There was a total eclipse earlier this year," said Alice. "Do you remember, Rob? We watched it through the conservatory roof at school. Everything went eerily quiet and cold. I think the birds stopped singing for a few moments."

"Yes. I remember. So what have you got to give us, then?" said Robert.

King Canute reached inside his tunic.

"The amber marbles," he said.

He opened his hand and four translucent orange stones tumbled onto the grass.

"Time Triggers?" said Robert and Alice in unison.

The king nodded.

"The runestones tell of their first discovery in Baltic lands many hundreds of years ago. They were used by the Celtic druids in Britain and have passed to me since my holy men interpreted the writings on the standing stones."

Alice thought the young man almost smirked. His bright eyes glowed.

"I am the rightful King of England. I have become a Christian, with the blessing of His Holiness in Rome. It is my duty to unite the kingdoms of Mercia, Anglia, Northumbria and Wessex. Already, under my leadership, my English subjects have prospered like never before. We trade and grow rich and secure. A comet hailed the new millennium and many said it would be the end of our world. But it was not. My laws have united this kingdom that has for centuries been ravaged by invaders from all over Europe."

"But you are a Viking, aren't you?" said Robert.

"Viking? A sea raider? Ha!" Canute laughed. "How ignorant you are! Your history teachers need to get their facts right. I am no raider. My love for this kingdom is true. I am the king. I am no more a foreigner than the Angles and Saxons. This island is part of my empire now and I am the divine king. My son is the true successor."

"So why do you need our help?" said Alice.

"Many wait in the wings to kill my son. This land still heaves with the memories of the bloodfeuds that have torn its leadership apart for generations.

My son is in Denmark, but he will sail to these shores to claim his throne. It is written on the runestones that I should come here to you and pass on the marbles. Only you have the power to fulfill the ancient prophecy. In their wisdom, the Spirits of Time have chosen you. Perhaps they were wise. By using travellers from a new millennium they knew they could protect the laws of time from the dark souls of this age. It has been translated from what is written on the stones that whoever receives the marbles from you will secure the crown of all England and that the succession will pass on to the descendants of this one true king. The magic in these charms will thus protect my son and the kingship of this land."

King Canute stood up. Keeper lifted his head at the disturbance to his snooze.

"Time is short," said Canute. "You must use the marbles to find my son when his ships land here and give them to him. But first, you must visit my wife, Queen Emma. She is a time traveller and knows of the runestones' prophecy about you. She will help you to fend off the usurpers and she will give you back the fourth marble that I must now use to travel back."

"Do you know that you will die soon then?" asked Robert.

"I think it is likely. But death holds no fear for me." The king grew taller. His eyes flashed with power. "My concern is for my successor. You must make sure that my son is the one true king."

Canute re-arranged his weapons on his belt.

"I must go now," he said. "I have a show for your ancestors! They need to know that I am a man. I have done much for them and some think me a God instead of their king. I will go down to the beach

24

and prove to them that the tide will not turn back for me!" Canute cackled. "Oh...beware of the Normans. For now, they are loyal, but there are some who consider they have a claim to the English throne."

Canute stooped and picked up one of the amber marbles.

"I will close the Time Tunnel. You can watch, but you two are still novices and you will need to grow up before you can command this power!" said King Canute, leaning over to the lustrous tube wall.

Canute touched the wall with the Time Trigger. He stretched up, dragging a string of light over his head, muttering an ancient chant. When his arm and the Trigger touched the ground on his other side, there was a brilliant flash of light. Alice was forced to close her eyes. When she opened them, the man had gone.

Keeper barked madly.

"It's O.K. boy," said Alice, stroking the dog to calm him. She was shaking and dizzy.

Robert walked over to where King Canute had been and examined the grass.

"Look, Alice. The grass is burnt where he touched it," he said.

"Somehow, that doesn't surprise me," said Alice. "And the tunnel wall has gone."

She gently picked up the three remaining amber stones. A cold chill flushed through her.

"Oh, dear," she said, holding the translucent objects in the palm of her hand. "Here we go again ...another quest!"

4

Cragg's Café

"So, you've heard of King Canute," said Robert as they walked back.

"Umm. Yes. I have," said Alice. "He's quite famous around here. According to legend, he once held back the sea. But from what he's just said, he probably didn't. He tried to, but failed, to prove a point to the people."

"Sounds like a publicity stunt to me," said Robert. "That guy is no fool. He looks clever and violent."

"He needs our help, though," said Alice. "According to the prophecy we're the only ones who can guarantee kingship with these Time Triggers. It sounds like there could be people waiting to get Canute or his son."

"You're good at history, Alice," said Robert. "When did Canute reign and who DID become king after him, according to our history books?"

"Umm. Well...he was a Viking, whatever he says. And Vikings came well after the Romans...but before William the Conqueror."

"The 1066 William?" said Robert.

"Yes, like we've been doing in history. The battle of Stamford Bridge was before the battle of Hastings, but only just. I think Canute was before that, but not much. He said it himself...just after the year 1000. The last millennium."

"So when were people like Alfred the Great, Ethelred the Unready and Edward the Confessor?" said Robert.

"I think they were all in the same era...the

26

Anglo-Saxons," said Alice.

"So when were the Vikings? Come on Alice!"

"I'm doing my best! Those were the Dark Ages, because no one really knows what happened then. Nobody wrote anything down."

Robert raised his eyebrows impatiently.

"I think...but I'm not absolutely sure...," said Alice. "...that the Vikings were in between all those. I think the Danes kept invading all through that period. They had a final try at the Battle of Stamford Bridge, didn't they? We know that from last week's lesson. Earl Tostig swapped to their side to try to beat his brother, King Harold, didn't he?"

"But according to the history I know, William the Conqueror invaded England and became king," said Robert. "Does that mean our quest is to change all that, if Canute's descendants get to keep the crown?"

"Maybe it does. Perhaps we've got to put history right," said Alice.

"Power, or what?" said Robert, grinning.

"Umm. Unless..."

"Unless what?"

"Unless we've got to protect these amber marbles from all the others who are after it until we can give them to William," said Alice.

"Give them to William the Conqueror? Canute didn't say anything about that," said Robert.

"Well, he wouldn't, would he?" said Alice. "He wants us to pass them on to his son and make him king. We'd better keep our wits about us, Rob, 'til we know a bit more."

"I'm starving," said Robert. "I can't think when I'm this hungry. Shall we go back and see if your Nan has done the bacon butties yet?"

"Good idea," said Alice. "What shall we do with these three Time Triggers for now?"

"Shall I take one and you keep two?" said Robert.

Alice nodded. She passed a marble to Robert and they put them in their pockets. Alice glanced up at the hulk of windmill and smiled. This wonderful place was really special now.

They walked back to the bungalow, chatting excitedly about Dark Age kings and a neat little trick called a Time Tunnel and how many rashers of bacon Nan would put into their breakfast.

They were not disappointed.

"Six rashers!" pronounced Robert joyfully, before clamping his jaws around the crispy roll.

"Nan?" said Alice.

"Yes, pet?"

"Do you know anything about King Canute?"

"Aye. He lived hereabouts. A long time ago, mind," said Nan. She was standing at the kitchen sink, the butt of a cigarette clamped in the corner of her mouth as she spoke. The bow on her apron wobbled on her ample frame as she scrubbed at the dirty dishes. "I don't know much more than that, though."

Alice frowned with disappointment.

"Cedric does though," added Nan.

"Cedric?" said Alice.

"Mr Cedric Godwineson. He lives in the shack behind the lifeboat shed on the beach. He's a bit of a hermit most of the time. Lots of rumours about him. Some say he's a druid. Some say he's a hundred and ten. Lot of nonsense! He knows a lot about the history of these parts and he plays a good hand of whist on Thursday nights down at *The King's Arms!*" Nan laughed. It made her cough.

Alice and Robert looked at each other. A thrill stirred inside Alice. This Mr Godwineson sounded fascinating.

"Can we meet him?" asked Robert.

Nan pulled out the plug and turned round. A sly grin twisted the empty corner of her mouth.

"Don't see why not," she said. She looked up at the old pine kitchen clock and winked at Alice. "He'll be having his pie and chips in Cragg's Café at one o'clock. Maybe you could run my letters down to the village post office in a bit and call in at the café."

Alice and Robert nodded enthusiastically.

"The horses are back in the field next door, Alice. There's a foal now," said Nan.

"Oh, wow! Can we go and look?" said Alice.

"Of course! Be off with you, the pair of you!" said Nan, shooing them through the back door with a tea towel.

"Oh ... sorry," said Alice, looking at Robert's half smile. "You're not into horses, are you?"

"I like horses. They're cool," said Robert. "I'm not really great with any animals though. Never had a pet."

Alice thought he looked a bit sad.

"Well, you're O.K. with Keeper," she said.

Right on cue, Keeper came bounding around the side of the house, carrying an old shoe. He dropped it at Robert's feet and looked up at him with his big, brown eyes.

"He wants you to pick it up and throw it for him," said Alice.

Robert bent over and Keeper's body quivered in anticipation. He barked.

"It's O.K.," said Alice. "If he grabs one end and pulls on the shoe, just pull harder. He loves that!"

After a couple of throws, Robert grinned proudly. Keeper sped off, retrieved the crumpled leather and dropped it at Robert's feet every time. Robert patted Keeper's shiny, flat coat more aggressively and teased the delighted dog with fake throws before hurling the shoe across the garden again.

"We don't really know what we're supposed to do in this quest, do we?" said Alice.

"Travel back and give the amber marbles to Canute's son, I thought?" said Robert, fighting with Keeper.

"Yes. Probably. But where and when?"

"Umm. See what you mean. We'd better not guess or we could end up somewhere we don't want to be," said Robert. He threw the shoe again.

"This Mr Cedric Godwineson might be able to tell us a bit more about when King Canute was here. I've got a feeling that Mr Cedric is part of all this, somehow," said Alice.

Robert raised his eyebrow. "Umm. You and your feelings have been right before. Shall we see if Nan has got those letters ready yet?"

Alice nodded eagerly. Thankfully, Nan had finished.

"Here, pet," said Nan. She pushed a five-pound note into Alice's hand. "Buy yourselves something at the café." She winked at Alice.

Alice kissed her grandmother and set off with Robert and Keeper down the lane, past the turn off to the windmill and into the village of Canewdon.

"She's great, your Nan," said Robert.

"I know," said Alice. "Now where's the café...ah, ha! I remember now. Over there. Look."

Cragg's Café was a tiny place with short net curtains across the bottom of the steamy front window. The glass was covered with notices displaying this week's special offers, as well as a variety of items being offered for sale by local residents. Alice tied Keeper to a rusty iron loop beside the entrance and Robert pushed open the door. A bell tinkled inside.

It took a moment to adjust to the dim interior. Alice couldn't help thinking the owners wouldn't need the lights on if there were fewer notices stuck on the window.

There were groups of people eating and drinking in the café. One or two stopped talking to inspect the newcomers. A man sat alone in the corner reading a newspaper, with his back to the shop. Alice thought she saw his shoulders stiffen as they walked up to the counter. Alice glanced over at him. She stifled a gasp. The newspaper man was watching them in the reflection of the mirror in front of him. Her eyes met his and she drew her breath. There was something familiar in his expression.

His eyes were almost black and seemed to smile without moving. A squashed hat lurked above his bushy eyebrows and beard. His jacket was old and tatty and a bit too big for him. Alice half expected him to be wearing fingerless gloves, but she saw that his hands were smooth and clean as he folded the newspaper onto the table beside him.

Robert prodded her.

"Which one?" said Robert.

"Which one what?" said Alice.

"Weren't you listening?" said Robert, frowning. "We can have either lemonade or blackcurrant. That's all they've got."

"Oh . . . lemonade is fine, thanks," said Alice.

The chubby lady in a checked apron nodded and disappeared back into the kitchen.

"Shall we ask about Nan's friend when she comes back?" said Robert.

"Er, if you like. But I think I know him already."

"You do?" said Robert. He followed Alice's gaze. "Him? Are you sure?"

"Yes. I'm sure."

"Shall we..."

But Alice was already walking over to the table. She walked round to the empty bench seat against the wall and faced the man.

"Mr Godwineson?" she asked.

The man nodded and stood up. He offered Alice his hand.

"You are Alice. And this must be Robert," he said, as Robert appeared at Alice's side. "At last we meet. Now...it can begin."

5

Time Regent

Alice and Robert stared at Mr Cedric Godwineson.

"Are these two joining you?" asked the jolly waitress. She put their glasses on the table.

"Indeed they are," said Cedric.

"That's just a pound, then, for the drinks," said the waitress.

Alice reached into her pocket for the money Nan had given them. But Cedric paid the lady before she had time to find the five-pound note.

"Allow me," said Cedric. "Please... take a seat. I think you may have a few questions for me. Am I right?"

"How did you know?" said Alice.

"It is the job of a Time Regent to see what needs to be done. When the time comes for a traveller to undertake a quest and we are needed, we wait in the chosen place until we are contacted."

"A *Time Regent?*" said Robert.

"Yes. That is my title. A Time Regent is a traveller with great powers, my friends. A Regent is one of the chosen ones who can travel across the chasms of time, just like you, but who has developed his or her powers with experience," said Cedric. "We Regents are the chief guardians of the highways of time, commissioned by the spirits to protect other time travellers and ensure that their quests are not corrupted by evil. Now then, young friends, I presume you have met King Canute?"

Robert nodded.

"Has he given you something... perhaps I should

say *things?*" said Cedric.

"How do we know that we can trust you?" said Alice.

Cedric smiled at her.

"How do you know that you can trust Canute?" he said.

Alice frowned.

"I don't think we know enough about the quest to decide yet," said Alice.

"A wise reply, young traveller. May I tell you a story?" said Cedric.

"I think you're going to, anyway," said Robert.

The bearded man threw back his head and laughed.

"You two make a formidable team, I can see that," he said. "Let me begin. Close your eyes and imagine. Imagine this island, this Britain, as it was at the dawn of the last millennium. In case you did not know, King Ethelred was the English king in the year 1000. Historians have named those times the Dark Ages. But the skies were no less blue and the countryside was a great deal greener than now. This was a rich and fertile island. Anglo-Saxons minted coins of silver unrivalled in the rest of Europe. Small wonder then, that its Scandinavian neighbours sent fleets of warships filled with young men eager to take some for themselves.

"It was also a time of treachery and greed within the rich Anglo-Saxon families of this island. Leaders switched allegiance to their former enemies and back again, to survive. Royal execution and murder was commonplace.

"The ordinary folk saw so many changes in their feuding leaders in one generation that they dreaded the thunderous approach of another conquering army, be it Saxon or Viking. In this Anglo-Scandinavian world, they preferred only the leader who could bring about calm, so that they might resume their lives in peace. And then, came Canute."

Cedric's half-smiling eyes looked at Alice and Robert in silence for several moments.

"Have you seen these things for yourself?" said Alice, eventually.

"Yes," said Cedric. "And so will you."

Robert grinned at Alice.

"Is there more to your story, then?" said Alice.

"Ah, yes...Canute," sighed Cedric. "He was a bold and clever youth. A Danish prince. A Viking. He was violent and ruthless too with a reputation for slaughtering his enemies mercilessly. His thirst for conquest brought him victory. Having conquered much of England by force, the remaining Saxon leaders accepted Canute as king. He was still hardly more than a boy."

"But why would the English accept a foreign king?" said Alice.

"In part, because of his mighty armies and in part because he became a Christian like them," said Cedric. "And then, he married Emma."

"Was that a smart move?" said Robert.

"Oh, yes. Very clever. Emma was King Ethelred's widow," said Cedric. "And now we're getting close to when you come into it."

Alice and Robert glanced at one another.

"Go on then, tell us," said Robert.

"Well, during a visit to Essex, not far from here, on a hill close to the site of one of his battles, Canute found the runestones and next to them, the amber marbles, as was his destiny. It is not known how they got there. According to the prophecy, Canute would find them and be charged to guide you two to your own destiny. His advisors read the ancient runes and he came to realise the power of the objects he had chanced upon. He began to travel the highways of time."

"He's like us then?" said Robert.

"Um, well, he is a time traveller." Cedric's face darkened and his eyes narrowed.

"What are you not telling us?" said Alice. "There's something wrong, isn't there?"

"Canute has his own agendas. He is corrupting the magic of the marbles for his own gain. He and Emma had a son. They named him Harthacanute. Canute had found the amber marbles not long after the boy was born. Whether it was deliberate, or whether it was a poor translation, Canute ignored the true meaning in the ancient runes. Canute is up to mischief. I would like to know what he has asked you two to do."

"According to our history books, William the Conqueror became the true king," said Alice.

"Precisely so, my child," said Cedric. "And you must give me the amber marbles so that I can ensure that history continues as it should."

"Hang on," said Robert suddenly. "How do you know all this? And how do we know it's not you that's up to mischief?"

The bearded man smiled.

"Come outside, and I will show you," said Cedric, rising from his chair.

"How old do you think he is, Alice?" whispered Robert as they swigged the last of their drinks and followed him out of the shop.

"I was wondering that myself. He looks old, but his hands aren't wrinkled, and he moves very quickly," said Alice.

She untied Keeper. Cedric ruffled the dog's fur affectionately behind one of his ears but Keeper gave a low growl.

"Sshh, Keeper!" said Alice. "Cedric is a friend."

The mysterious man led them along the promenade and down some sandy steps onto the beach. Sea gulls cawed gently above them over the rise and fall of the waves. The sea breeze wafted the delicate salty smell of the ocean towards them. They followed Cedric along the beach. It wasn't easy walking on the sand in trainers, but Cedric didn't seem to be having any difficulties in his blue boating shoes. The laces weren't even tied up. Keeper tugged on his lead but Alice didn't let him off. She was glad the dog was with them and that there were plenty of other people around.

After a few hundred yards, Cedric stopped under the overhanging dunes and pulled aside a matted door. It was well camouflaged and unlikely to be seen by other beach users.

"Stay here," said Cedric, and he disappeared. The door flapped back across the small opening after him.

"Now what?" whispered Robert.

"Dunno. Does he remind you of anyone?" said Alice.

Robert thought for a moment.

"You mean Eidor the Shaman, who we met in France, don't you?" he said.

"Yes!" said Alice. "I bet he was a Time Regent too."

Cedric re-emerged through the flap.

"Right. Found what I need. Let's sit down again shall we," he said. He sat down cross-legged. Robert and Alice fidgeted until they were comfortable on the sand.

"I overheard mention of a Time Regent in France. You called him a shaman. He was like me. You can trust me. I suppose I am a kind of shaman, really. I don't really care what label I am given by the people of your time. We Regents are nomads in time and space. We roam the universe until we are called to intervene if there are travellers in difficulty. Then we blend into the community and wait. You have met others and will go on to cross paths with many more, if your destiny holds true. Perhaps, with the collected wisdom of many travels, you may even become Time Regents yourselves someday."

Robert swallowed hard.

"Not sure I fancy being a nomad. I quite like it in my own time," he said.

"Time is not yours to own. Free will is yours, but you must learn to see, in order to make better choices. There are ways of seeing."

"I'm not blind," said Robert.

"Looking and seeing are not the same, my young friend. Look up there at that tree. What do you see?"

"A tall, brown tree with leaves and bits of roots showing," said Robert.

"Is that all?" said Cedric.

"Well, there is some rubbish caught up in the roots," said Robert.

"I see a world within a world," said Cedric. "A microcosm of pathways. I see movement and contour. Life and death. Parasites sap the tree's energies. Other creatures live in harmony. The sand is kept from erosion by the roots and the birds find shade beneath its leaves."

Robert pursed his lips and frowned. He looked back at the tree for a moment. Then he smiled.

Cedric raised his hand.

"Enough of that for the present. I must convince you that you can trust me. Let me show you something," he said.

In his other hand he held a large conch shell. It was pure white with salmon pink tips on the spiny projections.

"This is the Shell of Destiny," said Cedric. "It came into my possession on a very different beach on far away shores in a distant age. It has the power to show you what you must do."

6

The Shell of Destiny

Cedric the Time Regent lifted the shell to face the sea and held it still for a few moments. Then he started chanting in a low, melodious voice.

Alice watched the shaman, feeling just a hint of embarrassment in case anybody was looking at them.

In a sudden sweeping movement, Cedric lowered the shell and scooped some sand. Still chanting, he raised the shell over his head and down to the beach on the other side. A thread of sand traced an arched window in front of him. Robert gaped and Alice forgot where she was completely. The fine trail of grains sparkled in the sunlight. Keeper briefly lifted his head, then went back to his dozing.

As Alice watched, to her amazement, the window beneath the thread of sand transformed into glass. Then she saw movement on it.

"Wow! That's beautiful!" she said. "It's like a photograph negative."

"Look and see, my friends," said Cedric.

As Alice and Robert watched, the players on the screen became clearer.

"It's King Canute," said Alice.

"Who's the lady with him?" said Robert.

"That's Queen Emma," said Cedric, from the other side of the screen.

"What are they looking at in her hand?" said Robert. "Oh, hang on . . . they're the amber marbles. Pity we can't hear what they're saying."

"Look and see," said Cedric.

"And who is this?" said Alice.

The first scene was fading. The image of a handsome young man crouching on the ground became stronger and easier to look at. A horse was tethered in the background.

"That's someone else," said Robert. "He looks younger."

"Ah, yes. This vision comes to me often. His name is Edwin of Mercia. His grandmother was Lady Godiva."

"It's changing again," said Alice.

"Ships! Lots of them," said Robert. "They're not Viking longships though. Where are they going?"

"These belong to a powerful invasion force that seeks to conquer this island. They are landing on the shores of England and their leader will seek to defeat the reigning king," said Cedric. "Can you guess who they are?"

Alice suddenly knew.

"The Normans!" she cried.

"Exactly," said Cedric.

"Them too?" said Robert. "We've got to take the Normans on as well?"

He gave Cedric a 'you-must-be-joking' look.

"No," said Cedric.

"Phew," said Robert sarcastically.

"But..." said Cedric.

"Uh, oh!" said Robert.

"...the outcome of the invasion at Hastings is in your hands," said Cedric.

"Oh. Nothing big, then," said Robert.

Alice took a deep breath.

"What do we have to do?" she said.

The picture in the window vanished and the sparkling thread collapsed into a fine mist and settled back invisibly on the beach. A few grains landed on Keeper's nose. He twitched and snorted.

"Where are the amber marbles?" said Cedric.

Robert patted his jeans pocket and Alice pointed to hers.

"I take it I have convinced you that I mean you no harm?" said Cedric.

The others nodded.

"Show me the marbles," he said.

With a quick glance at one another, Alice and Robert brought out the orange stones.

"Three? Is that all?" said Cedric. His confident expression slipped into a chilling glower.

"He used the fourth one to close the Time Tunnel and took it back with him," said Alice.

"Canute used a Time Tunnel?" said Cedric, surprised. "His powers have advanced. This is more serious than I thought."

He closed his eyes in silence. The other two looked at each other.

"Right, then," said Cedric, opening his eyes again. "Tell me exactly what he asked you to do, please."

"Well, he said we needed to travel back to speak to Emma, who would give us the fourth marble and help us get them all back to his son, didn't he?" said Robert, looking at Alice.

"Yes," she said. "That's about right. And that whoever we pass the amber marbles to will be crowned king of all England."

"The true line of future kings and queens will indeed be determined by your actions, young friends," said Cedric. "But there are several time travellers who are aware of this prophecy. Some seek to corrupt the power of the Time Triggers and alter the true course of history. Canute I know about. There are others. I have seen shadows lurking. You will need to resist tyranny. Now that the quest has been awoken, you can expect more visits, I fear."

"So, what do you suggest we do?" said Robert. "Wait around until that happens?"

"No. You must retrieve the fourth marble and then bring them all to me. I will help you complete your task," said Cedric. "I think perhaps you should visit Emma."

"What happens if we give the amber marbles to the wrong person?" said Alice.

"According to the prophecy, all future heirs will touch the marbles, however fleetingly, but it is up to you to pass all four to the true king, who will keep them safely. The runestones testify that if others take them and try to use them for their own purposes or to alter their destiny, they may be cursed with death," said Cedric. He scoffed slightly.

"Are you saying that *all* heirs to the English throne must touch these triggers?" said Robert.

"No," said Cedric. "The Time Triggers have surfaced for a specific quest at the turn of the last millennium. From what I have seen in my visions, this quest will be decided on the battlefield at Hastings. By then, the amber marbles will have played out their hand in the game of life and their power as Time Triggers will cease. The outcome of that battle will be determined by the intrigues and events that precede it. It is your part in these events that will decide the fate of those involved."

"Cool!" joked Robert. But his eyes belied his fears.

Alice felt a bit queasy.

"Where do we have to time travel from, to meet up with Queen Emma?" she said.

She really did feel sick now.

"I think you have your answer, my friend," said Cedric. "The spirits have activated the Triggers. I will wait for you. Bring me all four marbles."

Alice looked across at Robert and knew that he was travelling too. Just too late, she remembered Keeper. She watched him fade into a far off beach as she felt herself sucked up into a whirl of white. She closed her eyes and concentrated on the face of the queen she had seen through the arched window. When she felt the warmth of soft sand beneath her knees, she opened her eyes.

It was night on the beach. A dense fog swirled about her, so thick that she could not see the sea. But she could hear it beyond her bubble of visibility. As she crept along the beach, her bubble moved with her. Beyond her bubble there was only darkness and fog. Alice peered into the mists and called quietly for Robert. He was nowhere to be seen.

7

Longship

"Where are you, Rob?" said Alice, in a loud whisper.

Only silence replied. Her heart started to quicken. Then she heard men's voices, in the distance at first, but quickly getting louder through the fog. And there was another sound, like a regular splashing. Then she saw it.

Its face was red and it had yellow horns. It had huge fanged teeth and evil black eyes. Alice gasped and staggered back to the cliff wall beneath the overhanging sand dunes. Still it kept coming, as high as a house, looming fearfully from the edge of the fog.

Hardly able to breathe for the fear that gripped her, Alice started to make sense of what she was seeing. It was the figurehead on the high prow of a Viking longship. It slowed to a halt, uncomfortably close to Alice. The overlapping oak planks of the hull grated on the pebbles. The fog retreated slightly. Along the longship, Alice watched oars being pulled inside the boat through holes near the top. Colourful round shields decorated the sides of the boat. Sailors pulled on the sealskin ropes and the mighty red and white striped sail began to fold.

The boat was tethered to a wooden jetty that extended twenty metres or so into the sea. Alice began to make out the silhouettes of a few timber-framed houses built higher up the cliff. She waited in the shadows until most of the men had disembarked. Then she started to edge along the cliff towards the jetty. There was still no sign of Robert.

There were steps leading up from the beach. Alice hesitated. Was she invisible? She should be, unless anyone had time travelling powers. She was a novice at time travelling and there were still many aspects of its lore that she knew she did not understand. She took a deep breath and decided she had to try. Slowly, Alice climbed the wooden steps.

The jetty was busy. Men and women were unloading barrels and baskets from the boat. Geese and chickens squawked as they dived to avoid rushing feet. Alice wrinkled her nose at the strong, unfamiliar smells.

The girls and women wore long woollen shifts and a second apron layer. The shoulder straps were fastened with brooches and they had plaited their hair or wore scarves. The men and boys wore breeches and knee-length tunics and many had leather straps lacing their boots right up to the knee. Some wore cloaks and most of the men had beards. No one seemed to notice Alice. She crept off the jetty.

The thatched houses of the cliff top settlement were built on either side of a timbered pathway.

"Psst!"

Alice jumped.

"Oh, it's you. Thank goodness!" she said, as she recognised Robert beckoning to her from the side of one of the houses. "Have you been up here since we arrived?"

"Yes. I wondered where you were. Did you see that longship docking? It was spectacular!"

"Yes I DID!" said Alice. "I was still down on the beach. It nearly ran me down!"

"Cool!" said Robert.

"Shall we look around?" said Alice. "We need to find this Queen Emma somewhere. Let's try walking down the path further inland."

"Sounds good to me," said Robert. "Keep in the shadows, just in case anyone sees us."

There was a bigger merchant's house further down the path. Cooking smells wafted out through the entrance with the music of panpipes and harp.

"We may as well start here," said Alice.

In the great hall, a large group was feasting. Flattened loaves of bread and a variety of meats were on offer. Most people ate with their hands or used a dagger. There were jugs of sweet smelling mead. Some men swigged wine from drinking horns.

But the lady at the head of the table was not eating. She was looking straight at Alice and Robert.

"Queen Emma," breathed Alice.

"Result or what!" said Robert.

"She doesn't look too pleased to see us, though," said Alice.

Queen Emma stood up slowly. She walked gracefully around the noisy table and the fire that roared in the central hearth.

"I think she's the only one who is a time traveller and can see us," said Alice.

"Can't say I'm sorry," said Robert. "The rest look a lot bigger than us!"

Queen Emma paused to look at Alice and Robert. She beckoned to them. They followed her. Alice noticed her beautiful brooches and necklaces. The central gems were mounted in etched metal. They passed through a curtained doorway into a bedchamber.

"Greetings," said Emma. She had a soft French accent. "I knew it would be soon. You have seen my husband?"

"Canute has spoken to us, yes," said Robert.

"Do you have the marbles then?" said Emma. She looked furtively through the doorway behind them.

"Maybe," said Robert. "But we have a few questions for you first."

Queen Emma stared at Robert with steely grey eyes. She was older than Alice had expected. Then Alice had an idea. Perhaps Canute had died and Harthacanute was grown up already.

"What year is this?" asked Alice.

"1036," said Emma.

Alice was still confused.

"Is your husband, Canute, still king?" she asked.

Queen Emma shook her head.

"No. He died last year."

"Then who is king?" asked Robert.

"No-one," said Emma.

The others frowned at each other in confusion.

"How is that possible?" said Robert. "Someone has to be king, don't they?"

"The lords of this island cannot agree on who," said Emma. Again, she looked fearfully behind into the dining hall. "One of most powerful of them, Earl Godwine of Wessex, is back in there. For the moment, he is my ally. He supports me in my quest to keep the title for my son."

"Harthacanute?" said Alice.

"Yes. He has been detained in Denmark, warding off the threat from Norway, but he is on his way here. There are those who would usurp him. Saxons! But according to the prophecy on the runestones, the true king must be of Norman blood. I am a Norman, so Harthacanute is the true king."

"Do you have the fourth marble?" said Alice.

"No. I trust it is safe with my son."

She spoke curtly to the children.

"Give me the other marbles. I will give them to my son so that he can condemn his enemies and triumph!"

Robert and Alice looked at one another.

"Is this what we must do?" said Alice.

Robert shrugged his shoulders and took out his Time Trigger. The orange gem sparkled in his palm.

"This doesn't feel right," said Alice. "I think we have to give the Time Triggers to the king himself."

"No! Give them to me!"

Queen Emma drew a dagger from her waistband.

"Oops," said Robert, as both he and Alice took a big step backwards. "Maybe we should use the Triggers?"

Just as Alice was about to agree with him, she felt herself pushed back by a gust of air. In a dazzling flash, they were joined by someone else, someone who could time travel and appear from nowhere.

8

Edwin of Mercia

The young stranger staggered and blinked, adjusting to his new surroundings. He was standing in the doorway. Queen Emma retreated with her back against the wall. The young man was older than Alice and Robert, cloaked and dressed for combat. But his were not the clothes of a Viking.

"The boy from the arched window," said Alice.

Robert was nodding.

"Hello," said the young man, with a slight bow. "We have not yet had the pleasure of acquaintance. I am Edwin of Mercia and you two are distant kinsfolk from a future age, I believe. I will elaborate later. For now, it looks as if I have arrived exactly as I was warned to. I hope you have not surrendered the amber marbles, my friends?"

Alice shook her head. Robert looked confused and impatient. He was still holding his Time Trigger in the palm of his hand.

"Madame," said Edwin, addressing Queen Emma. "I know what you have planned, but it is not to be. I have already taken your son's Trigger while he slept. It was never his to keep."

Queen Emma's eyes glared with hatred. Suddenly, she opened her mouth and gave a furious scream.

"Saxon scum!" she yelled.

But she was no match for a warrior. Edwin flung his cloak over his shoulder and grasped Emma's wrists. She winced in pain and dropped the dagger, bellowing a tirade of French abuse. She kicked out at him.

"Get out of here, my friends," said Edwin over

Emma's shoulder. "This noise is going to attract unwelcome company." He gestured towards the doorway with his head. Alice could already hear the sounds of chairs being pushed backwards and footsteps approaching.

She nudged Robert and they fled through the door, dodging invisibly around the crowd of running men.

"Good job they couldn't see us!" panted Robert, as they ran out of the house and down the roadway towards the edge of a forest.

They stopped in a clearing to get their breath back.

"Wonder what happened to our new friend in there?" said Alice.

"He is a time traveller. He should be O.K.," said Robert. "He must have a Time Trigger. He'll use that."

"Um. Wonder what Time Trigger?" said Alice.

"The one I want back!" said a voice.

"Oh, no! Not more trouble!" said Robert, springing round. "Who are you, exactly?"

"My name is Harthacanute, time traveller and the rightful King of England."

The young man dismounted from his horse.

"Edwin of Mercia seems to dispute your claim," said Robert.

A ribbon of anger threaded across the young Viking's rugged features.

"I am King Canute's son. My mother, the Queen, is Emma of Normandy. In me, the royal line runs true, just as the runes foretold."

"You don't have a Time Trigger, do you?" said Alice.

"Ah! The fourth marble! It was stolen from me, by that Saxon! He can't possibly think *he* has a claim to the throne! The Godwine clan may well try to usurp me though. This Edwin is just a time travelling Mercian who must know of the prophecy. Unlike Earl Godwine, who would support whoever made his Wessex clan the richer, the Saxon Earl of Mercia does not favour a Danish claim to the throne of England. If the Mercians get their way, Queen Emma will soon be exiled, unless I get the Time Triggers back. First, I will have the three that you two children will surrender to me. And then Edwin's. With all four, I will be invincible!"

Harthacanute took a sudden step forwards and grabbed Alice. She was caught by surprise. He grasped her arms tightly across her chest.

Robert snatched a thick branch. He stepped towards Harthacanute, wielding the branch like a club.

"I don't think so!" laughed Harthacanute spitefully. "You need to do some training, BOY!"

Alice was thinking rapidly. In an inspired action of speed and cunning, she jolted her arms upwards, bringing the Danish boy's arm to her mouth, and bit hard into his flesh. At the same time, she swivelled slightly and stuck her knee into her attacker's groin.

The combination of pain was too much for Harthacanute, and he loosened his grip enough for her to force herself out, just as Robert deftly smacked his head with the tree branch. Harthacanute staggered backwards.

"Use a Trigger, Alice!" yelled Robert, lifting the club again.

9

A Terrible Discovery

Alice was already reaching into her pocket. She grabbed Robert's arm with her other hand and in a cloud of crystals and bright light, they were swept through time to the twenty-first century.

For a minute, they sat on the grass panting. Alice looked at Robert and they both burst out laughing.

"Poor guy!" spluttered Robert. "Wonder which bit of him hurts most!"

"Actually, you should have seen what you looked like when you swung that club around! Combination of *Tarzan* and *Fred Flintstone!*"

Robert pretended to look hurt, but spluttered into more giggles.

"Seriously," said Alice, trying to control herself. "What did we find out back there? We still have only three marbles."

"Emma said that the true king must be of Norman blood," said Robert.

"And we met that guy Edwin, who I don't think we've seen the last of, somehow. But we didn't give the Triggers to anyone," said Alice.

"Exactly," said Robert. He was more serious now. "We didn't. We've still got them, well, three of them, anyway. And at least we know a couple of people we *don't* want to give them to. I don't think we should surrender them to either Queen Emma, or her son."

"You mean we've narrowed down the list a bit?"

"Yes. I mean...everybody's charging about after these marble things aren't they?" said Robert.

"Yes. It is getting a bit busy in the time travelling world. I think we need to go back to the beach for Keeper and to ask Cedric's advice," said Alice.

"Yeah," said Robert. "And I'm getting really hungry too. What time is it?"

Alice glanced at her watch.

"Oops. Even if we haven't lost any modern time when we travelled, we must have been in that café and on the beach for a while. My aunt and uncle will be home from their shop soon. Better get back before they send out a search party."

They walked back along the cliff top path. The weather was changing. A cool wind blew grains of sand into their faces. The promenade was almost deserted. Brightly coloured beach huts now stood like faded soldiers along the edge of England, instead of the Viking settlement of the last millennium. Alice spotted a lone deckchair half way down the beach. Its red and white striped seat billowed in the breeze.

They walked down the concrete ramp onto the sand in front of the lifeboat hut. Alice heard a familiar bark.

"I'm coming, Keep!" she shouted.

They squeezed alongside the hut and reached a corrugated metal shack behind it. Smoke rose in a grey twist from the little chimney. The door was ajar. Robert knocked.

"Come in, friends," said Cedric.

He reached down from his armchair and untied Keeper. Alice braced herself for his canine greeting.

After hugs and licks for both children, Keeper finally calmed down and all three sat down in the only place available, on the rug by the fire.

"Cor! And my Mum thinks my room is untidy!" said Alice, glancing around her.

Every space in the single-roomed shack was covered by books, maps, charts or boxes. Hardly any carpet was visible. There was a well-worn track from the door to the little kitchen area and also to the fireside chair, and from there to the corner bed. But the rest of the floor and furniture was entirely covered by piles of things. A treasure chest with silver locks adorned one corner. Exotic vases, lamps and candlesticks were dotted here and there. A tapestry hung in the shadows. It was exquisitely embroidered. Cedric followed Alice's gaze.

"It's a fine piece of work, isn't it," he said. "It's medieval."

"What's the rocket thing flying across the top?" said Alice.

"That? It's a comet. People were very superstitious in the Dark Ages. They thought comets foretold of death. Do you see the ghostly figures? They foretold the death of a king."

"Which king?" said Robert.

Cedric shrugged his shoulders.

"Who knows? It's all myth and legend."

"It's beautiful," said Alice. "And I like the chest."

"Ah, that! A little something I picked up on my travels. Legend has it that it once contained a scroll written by Edward the Confessor describing a visit by an angel."

"Cool," said Alice.

"Now, tell me what happened just now," said Cedric.

He listened patiently while they took turns to describe their adventure. His face grew serious.

"Show me the amber marbles," he said.

Alice reached into her pocket and put her two Time Triggers on the rug in front of her. Robert fumbled in his pockets, one after the other.

"That's funny," he said. "I usually put it here... but... it must be here somewhere."

Alice frowned. She glanced at Cedric. His face was still as stone. His colourless eyes were fixed on Robert like bullets.

"I don't understand it," said Robert. He was beginning to panic.

"When did you last have it?" said Alice, trying to sound calm.

"Um... in the Viking chamber... then in the forest?"

He didn't look too sure.

"I used *my* Time Triggers to get us away from Harthacanute," said Alice. "You had both hands on the branch."

Robert stopped searching and looked guiltily at Cedric.

"Do you think you could have dropped it during the scuffle between Queen Emma and Edwin?" said Alice.

Robert looked really wretched now. He raised his hands in despair.

"You did," said Cedric calmly. "I saw it roll from your hand under Queen Emma's bed."

Alice and Robert stared at Cedric the Time Regent.

"Were you there?" said Alice.

"No," said Cedric. "I was looking into a sand window with the Shell of Destiny."

"Spying on us!" said Robert.

"If you like," said Cedric. "There are spies everywhere at the moment. Not all of them are friendly."

"Are you our friend?" challenged Robert aggressively.

"Of course I am!" shouted Cedric. He leapt up from his chair and started pacing backwards and forwards in front of the fire. "You must learn to take more care of your Triggers. They are not toys!"

"I'm sorry. I didn't realise..."

"Sorry is not enough. You must learn to discipline yourselves if you are to be trusted with these tasks. Never lower your guard...ever! Trust no one. Laugh if you like, and play, but never forget who you are...not even for a second! For that is when the agents of evil will strike. There is no time for carelessness and no time for laziness for the likes of us. The destiny of thousands is in your hands... under your protection. Do you understand me?"

Robert and Alice nodded meekly. Cedric looked very menacing. Alice felt her skin turn to goose-bumps. She also felt very sorry for poor Robert.

"He didn't mean to. He was saving me and..."

Cedric silenced her with his hand. His face melted into a liquid smile across his mouth and eyes.

"I know," he said. "I'm sorry I shouted. I think it is much to do with my own frustration. I know I have a part to play in this quest, but not yet. For now I must watch over you two. Come. Let us consider our options. We need a strategy."

He sat down again. Robert breathed a deep sigh and shrugged at Alice. She smiled back.

"You still have two marbles, and Edwin has one," said Cedric. He was deep in thought. "We have no idea who has the fourth. We...you...need to have all four."

"Maybe we should let whoever it is come to us," said Alice. "If they can, that is. They'll have to travel forwards."

"Yeah," said Robert. "I'd like to sort them out in our time, with our things! See how they'd like to fight in a busy town street with cars whizzing by!"

"I think you could be right, friends," said Cedric.

"I need to consult the Shell of Destiny. It is better done when I am alone. Perhaps you should go now, for a while. Return to your normal lives. But..." His voice grew serious again. "...do not lower your guard. Spies are everywhere."

10

Saxon in the Classroom

Robert stood up and took Keeper's lead. Alice scooped up the marbles from under Cedric's gaze and rammed them in her pocket.

"When shall we see you again?" she asked.

"I will find you, even if you go back to Mercia."

"Mercia?" said Alice.

"Oh, I forgot it is no longer called that. Mercia is now called the Midlands, really. Your hometown of Newark was in Mercia. Canute probably swept past Newark with his army on the way to York, when he conquered England in 1016. Earl Leofric was Earl of Mercia. Godiva, his wife, was one of the first owners of the Manor of Newark. Edwin, whom you have now met, was their grandson. You are Mercians. I am sure this is why you have been chosen for this quest."

"Is that the same Lady Godiva who rode though the streets without any clothes on?" said Robert, smirking slightly.

"Indeed, yes, young man. She did it for a bet with Leofric, you know. But enough of that. Ask Edwin when you see him. Go now. We will meet soon."

Alice and Robert said goodbye but Cedric did not answer them. His ashen face was fixed deep in thought.

"We really must get back to the bungalow," said Alice. "Keeper is late for his tea too, aren't you, boy?"

They raced back down the Essex lanes away from the sea. As she ran, Alice thought of how other feet had run through this place before. So many others over all the years of time. Marching armies perhaps. The trees had changed and the road was surfaced with modern tar now, but the space was the same. Like a giant cube of time. The constant block had witnessed the passing of so much life across the centuries.

"I'm so sorry I lost the Trigger," said Robert quietly as they slowed down on the driveway.

"Don't worry," said Alice. "Perhaps it was meant to be."

Robert considered this for a moment.

"Yeah. Perhaps it was," he said.

Alice's aunt and uncle were back from work. They were very welcoming. They ran a wallpaper and paint shop in the nearby town of Southend. Aunty Jane had brought fish and chips home for supper.

Robert and Alice managed to describe an afternoon spent on the beach and a chat about local history with Nan's friend in Cragg's Café without ever mentioning the exciting bits.

"Aren't grown ups easy to fool sometimes," said Robert, helping Alice to make up her camp bed for the night. "If you give them some details to think about they don't ask questions about the bits in between."

Alice grinned at him.

She didn't sleep very well that night. Apart from the scary dreams about shadowy figures, her grandmother snored loudly. And Nan got up early in the morning, just when Alice was slipping into deep sleep.

"Urgh! No lie-in this weekend," groaned Alice, trying to sneak another half an hour under the duvet.

She was woken again by Robert.

"Your Mum's here," he said, shaking her. "And we haven't seen Cedric again."

Alice sat up.

"Mum's early. Oh...nice jimmies!"

Robert looked a bit embarrassed.

"O.K. O.K. Racing car patterns aren't big at the moment. My Great Aunt Em bought these for me last Christmas. But they might be high fashion one day."

"Ha!"

"Well, ducks and rabbits on fleecy nighties aren't exactly cool either," said Robert.

Alice looked down and hastily pulled up the duvet.

"They're comfy though."

"Seriously," said Robert. "How are we going to see Cedric again, if we go back to Newark now?"

"He said to wait for him, didn't he?" said Alice, yawning. "He said he'd find us and I think he will. I think the clues for the rest of this mystery might be waiting for us back home."

"Hope you're right. I really want a chance to go back and get the other Triggers," said Robert.

But their chance didn't come that morning.

Alice's Mum stayed for coffee but wanted to get back home to collect Alice's little sister and get the homework and uniform sorted for Monday.

"I'll put you in my next English essay, Keep," whispered Alice, nuzzling Keeper affectionately. "And next time I come, we'll have a quiet time up at the windmill. I missed that this weekend."

"You take care now, lassie," said Nan.

"I'll try," said Alice.

"And bring this nice young man back to visit me again," said Nan. "You remind me of my Rich. That's Alice's grandad. He was a handsome man. He had legs for the kilt too. Is there any Scot's

61

blood in you, laddie?"

Robert looked down at his legs.

"Um...I don't think so."

"Och! Away with you, lad!"

The little silver car purred its way back up to Newark along the motorway.

"Wonder if we're in *Mercia* yet?" whispered Robert, smiling, as they crossed into Nottinghamshire.

"I've been thinking," said Alice, holding the two amber marbles in her hand. "Do you think you should have one of these while we're apart."

Robert pretended to nudge her, which would have pushed the Time Triggers onto the floor.

"Hey! Don't mess about, Rob!"

"Sorry."

Robert put on a mock sorry look.

"Do you want one or not?" said Alice.

Robert shrugged.

"It's O.K. You keep them for now," he said.

Alice's mum dropped Robert back home. His father was much better now and Mrs Davenport didn't look quite as stressed as before.

The evening dragged by and Alice went to bed early, partly because she was tired from lack of sleep the night before and partly because that way, tomorrow would come quicker.

Tomorrow became today and the frenzy of Monday morning distracted Alice until half way through the first lesson. It was science.

Alice was going off science, probably since they'd had to stop most practical lessons while the laboratories were housed in prefabricated classrooms outside, during the upgrading of the science block. Alice loved experiments. But learning lots of facts without them was hard. Mr Chillcott wasn't very inspiring either. His woolly jumpers were becoming the whispering point of the lessons.

He droned on about the properties of molecules when they were heated. Alice was half listening. She leant on one arm and wondered why the whole class couldn't get up in a long line and start bumping into each other from one end, like the heated particles. The bumping would spread along the line getting rougher as the heat was turned up. Now that would make a good experiment.

She noticed one of the boys perching on a side desk. She opened her eyes to see who was being so daring and she nearly fell off her own table in surprise when she recognised him.

Edwin of Mercia was sitting on the edge grinning at her, with one leather booted foot on the desk, hugging his leg against his red tunic. His sword lay casually on the table beside him.

11

Viking

Alice was stunned. She glanced automatically at Mr Chillcott, but she knew straight away that the teacher could not see Edwin. Then she slyly checked that Sarah was still scribbling notes next to her. She was.

Edwin was making faces at her now. He jumped off the side table and to Alice's horror, started walking towards Mr Chillcott. Alice drew her breath.

Her eyes bulged as Edwin stood directly behind the teacher and started to copy his movements. When Mr Chillcott lifted an arm, so did Edwin. If the teacher stepped forwards, Edwin followed him. Then he stuck his hands up like horns behind the teacher's head.

Alice spluttered a giggle. Sarah stopped writing and looked at her friend. Alice pretended to be coughing.

"Are you O.K?" asked Sarah.

At that moment, Edwin returned for his sword and stood behind a girl with an immaculately groomed hairstyle. It was Tessa, the self-appointed class queen. Edwin gently picked up the end of the girl's pony-tail and placed it on the blade of his sword. Alice nearly choked.

"Alice, what is it?" said Sarah.

She followed Alice's gaze, but saw nothing. Edwin replaced the pony-tail. He was standing behind Tessa, looking the model of innocence.

Alice relaxed slightly. She put up her hand.

"Yes, Alice?" said Mr Chillcott.

"Please may I go to the toilet, Sir?" she asked.

"Oh. And I thought you were going to stun us all with your views on the conduction of heat, Alice," said Mr Chillcott. "All right. All right. If you must."

Alice smiled at Sarah, who was frowning at her, and walked towards the door. She nodded towards Edwin, signalling for him to follow her. For a moment, the Anglo-Saxon teenager walked towards the blackboard. Alice glared at him furiously. Edwin pretended to sulk. Then he skipped after her.

Alice closed the door and let out a sigh of relief. She looked at Edwin and giggled.

"Hello again," said Edwin.

He swapped his sword into his left hand, swished back his cloak and shook Alice's hand warmly.

"What are you doing here?" said Alice, looking furtively around.

"Heard you might be in a bit of bother," said Edwin.

"What kind of bother?"

"The dangerous kind," said Edwin. "Deadly in fact. Someone wants what you and I have and they're on their way to get it."

"Who?"

"Harthacanute."

"Queen Emma's son?"

"One of them. She has two, don't forget. So many sons and so many pretenders!"

"Two?" said Alice.

"There is her first born..."

Edwin stopped as a boy carrying a register hurried past towards the school office. Alice ducked down and pretended to tie her shoelace.

"This way," she said, when the boy had gone. "We can't stay here."

Alice led Edwin down the school corridor. Each time they passed a classroom door, he peered in mischievously until Alice pulled him away.

"Funny smells in this place," said Edwin. "Sort of woody. I quite like it. It looks fun here. I wish such places had been around in my time. My tutor was a very boring fellow. All I wanted to do was go outside and practice my combat technique."

They passed the boys changing rooms.

"Oooh! Not sure I like that odour though!" said Edwin.

Alice nodded in agreement.

"Ah. Here's the geography room. Rob should be in here," said Alice.

She ducked below the window in the classroom door and peered over the sill to look for Robert. Miss Pearson, the geography teacher, was looking in her direction. Alice ducked down again.

"Allow me," said Edwin. "Your tutor will not see me. Now then...there he is. Umm. Need to attract his attention some how."

Edwin lifted his sword and pulled it up and down across the window. The sunlight reflected on the blade and Robert turned to look.

"He's seen us," said Edwin.

"Let me see," said Alice, peeping over the bottom of the window for a second.

Robert's eyes bulged in disbelief.

"Bet he's going to suddenly need a visit to the boys' changing rooms," said Alice, ducking back down and stifling a giggle.

Sure enough, two minutes later, Robert appeared through the doorway.

"Cool!" he said, shaking Edwin's hand. "An Anglo-Saxon in the school! To what do we owe this honour, then?"

"Shall we go outside and I will explain?" said Edwin. "We must hurry. There is not much time."

They found a bench around the side of the building, against the wall and well away from any open windows.

"Emma found the fourth marble, as I think you know. She has given it to Harthacanute," said Edwin.

Robert nodded, blushing slightly.

"Harthacanute is cursed of course, like all Canute's children, after their father's meddling in the prophecy. Like his half brothers and sisters, Harthacanute will die young from some mysterious disease. He knows he is on borrowed time, so he is searching for the rest of the marbles. He hopes that with the power of all four, he could become the rightful king. If that were to happen, he would change the course of history. Without the Time Triggers, he is certainly doomed."

"So he'll be here...any time now?" said Robert, looking around suspiciously.

"Yes!" said Edwin, standing up. "So, let's get ready, shall we? Do you have a horse?"

"A horse?" said Alice and Robert together.

Inside a bell rang. It was break time.

"I would not like to try to out run Harthacanute if he is on horseback," said Edwin.

"But we don't have horses anymore," said Alice. "Well, not for normal transport. We have cars."

"Cars? Well, can we ride *them*?" said Edwin.

"Umm, not really," said Robert. "We're too young. I sort of know what does what, but I'm not allowed to drive yet."

"Would your sheriff cast you into a dungeon or have you stoned for this offence?" said Edwin.

Robert and Alice looked at one another and

laughed. Edwin's mood changed. His playfulness switched to a mask of gravity.

"This is not a game, friends," he said. "Show me one of your cars, please."

Alice shivered uneasily. She heard rustling in the bushes and looked behind her. But there was nobody there. The door burst open and the children started to pour out. At least they were in a crowd now.

"This way," said Alice. She took Edwin's hand and led him across the netball court to the school gate.

"Cars!" she pronounced, pointing to the parked vehicles.

A small hatchback whizzed past at that moment. Edwin recoiled slightly at the unexpected noise and movement. Then a motorbike went the other way, followed by a van. Alice and Robert waited for Edwin's next move.

At that moment, they felt a cold wind in their faces and a shimmering glow grew stronger in the middle of the road in front of them.

Edwin gasped and grabbed the others by the arms.

"A Time Tunnel!" he said. "So his father has passed on the knowledge. This way, my friends!"

They turned and fled back through the school grounds. They ran around the perimeter of the playground and over the grass between the school building and the temporary science rooms. They paused behind the cold, corrugated metal and looked back around the corner. To Alice's horror, a Viking warrior was galloping around the playground on the back of a colossal horse.

12

Driving Lesson

The thunder from the horse's hoofs was very loud. Alice noticed that quite a few children had stopped chatting and were looking blindly in that direction. Mr Chillcott, who was on playground duty, looked up towards the sky as if expecting rain.

"Now what?" she said.

"Could we borrow that *car*?" said Edwin.

He was pointing at the caretaker's battered old camper van. The sliding side door was pulled open. The back was filled with paint pots, garden tools and dust sheets.

"Well, we can't stay here," said Robert. "Harthacanute will pulverize us. Let's go! I'll try and remember what to do. My dad let me drive the car in the driveway once."

They ran over to the van.

"I hope the keys are there!" muttered Alice.

"No! This side!" shouted Robert as Edwin started to climb into the passenger seat.

Luckily, the keys were in the ignition.

"Turn the key!" shouted Robert.

He pointed at the keys. Edwin copied Robert with his seat belt and started the engine.

"Put your foot on the accelerator pedal...no! That's the brake. The other one!" said Robert. "That's it. I'll push the gear into forwards and release the hand brake. Steer by turning the wheel the way you want to go. Now, GO!"

The van bucked and lurched forwards. The engine strained as Edwin pressed the accelerator pedal too hard. They shot towards the perimeter fence. Alice, who was sitting in the back amongst the paint and tools, was pushed back against her seat.

"Brake! The other pedal!" screamed Robert.

Edwin slammed his foot down and the van skidded to a halt. Alice grabbed for one of the ladders as she was catapulted forwards. Her seat belt kept her from hitting the back of Robert's chair.

"It's O.K. Don't worry!" said Edwin. "I think I've got it now. Hold on..."

He turned the steering wheel on full lock and they screeched in a tight circle to face the other way around, just as the grey horse and its rider turned the corner towards them.

The tall Viking horseman reined his steed to a halt. Van and horse faced each other for a moment. Edwin pushed aside his heavy sword and gripped the steering wheel. Alice held the side of her seat and half closed her eyes. With a whooping battle cry, Edwin pressed the accelerator. The camper van lurched forwards, straight towards Harthacanute and his horse.

The sight and sound of this metal horse of war coming towards it was too much for the horse. It reared high on its back legs, throwing Harthacanute to the ground, and bolted towards the bottom of the school playing field. It jumped the hedge easily and disappeared from view, into the urban jungle of the twenty-first century.

Edwin braked and the camper came to a standstill, just in front of Harthacanute. The Viking drew his sword.

"Leave him to me!" shouted Edwin. He leapt from the van and strode towards Harthacanute. He reached for his sword. "Where..."

He turned back, realising he had put it down in

the van. But Robert had not forgotten.

"On guard!" shouted Robert bravely, from the other side of the van.

Alice jumped down behind Robert.

"No, Robert!" she said. "He is a mighty king! You cannot defeat him."

"I know," hissed Robert. "But it gives you time to use the Time Triggers and get us out of here..."

Unfortunately for Robert, Harthacanute was advancing. In one mighty blow, he beat against Edwin's heavy sword, pushing it out of Robert's hand. He thrust his own Viking blade towards Robert's chest and stopped. For a moment, everyone stood very still.

A sly grin spread across the blond features of the Viking time traveller.

"To me," said Harthacanute.

He beckoned to Robert who had very little choice. Reluctantly he took a step towards his attacker. Harthacanute grabbed his arm and twirled Robert around in an arm lock. Pain swept across Robert's face.

Harthacanute pulled Robert closer with his bare, muscular arms.

"Give me your Time Triggers!" he ordered.

Alice looked across at Edwin in dismay.

"You know we cannot do that, Harthacanute," said Edwin calmly. "We are the guardians of these Triggers. We must reserve them for their true purpose."

"I am that purpose," said Harthacanute in his Scandinavian accent. "My mother was a Norman. I am the true king!"

"Yes. Canute thought that could be so," said Edwin. "And perhaps it might have been, if your father had not persisted in abusing the power of the amber marbles. Canute tried to corrupt the prophecy and ensure that *his* blood ran in the eternal lineage of the kings. Perhaps if he had not used the Time Triggers for his own power and advancement, he would not have incurred the wrath of the Spirits of Time and his bloodline would have run true. He knew he ran the risk of being cursed, but still he continued to meddle. That is why your brothers and sisters have all died young. And so will you. The successor's name is known. It has been revealed to a Time Regent. The spirits have chosen one of the pretenders. It is not you. The royal lineage must change."

"No! It is not so!" spat Harthacanute. He shook Robert. "Give me your Triggers, I say! Or I will kill your friend!"

Alice took her purple purse from the zipped pocket in her school skirt.

"No!" said Edwin. "We must be strong."

"These Time Triggers?" she said, wafting the purse about.

Harthacanute's eyes sparkled with greed.

"Throw them over to me!" he said.

"No!" protested Edwin and Robert together.

But it was too late. Alice hurled the little pouch high into the air. It landed in front of Harthacanute. He edged towards it, still gripping Robert. With his eyes on the other two, he stooped and fumbled on the ground. His fingers seized on the smooth leather.

Suddenly, Alice rushed towards Harthacanute. Edwin lunged forwards too. The force of the their weight pushed Harthacanute off balance and he fell backwards. Alice caught a glimpse of another orange object in Harthacanute's hand.

"Oh, no!" she cried.

Before she or Edwin could reach out for Robert, the air in front of them dazzled in a flare of light. Harthacanute vanished and so did Robert.

13

Blood Trail

Edwin was breathing hard.

"That was a foolish thing to do, Alice," he said. "Now he has three marbles. His powers will increase."

"But he doesn't have three marbles," said Alice.

She stood up and put her hand back in her skirt pocket. She pulled out her fist and opened her fingers. The two amber Time Triggers glittered in the sunlight.

"But..."

"All Harthacanute has got is my snack money for the cake shop."

Edwin roared with laughter.

"Clever girl, Alice. Were you hoping we could overpower him when we rushed at him?"

"Yes. Exactly. But I didn't count on him having the other Trigger in his hand."

"Brave try, my friend. I should have been quicker. Now we have a more complicated problem. We've got to go after Harthacanute for that fourth marble but we don't know exactly where he is."

"Hang on," said Alice. "He's got Robert, remember. And he's going to be mad when he opens that pouch. Robert's in great danger."

"More danger than you think," said Edwin. "Without a Time Trigger, Robert will be seen by all, wherever he is."

Alice's eyes widened with fear.

"We have to go back for him. Now. Come on!"

"Do you think you will be able to find them?" said

Edwin. "Are your powers pure?"

"Yes. I think so. I've always been able to go back to where I wanted, if I concentrate hard enough."

Edwin nodded.

"You will need great strength. Harthacanute will hide Robert well...or worse..." he said.

Alice swallowed hard and tried not to look as frightened as she was feeling.

"Harthacanute used a Time Tunnel to get here," she said. "But he used his Time Trigger in the normal way to go back. Is that possible?"

"Of course. To travel forwards in time *is* possible with a Time Trigger, as long as it is part of a quest and directed by the spirits. That is how I came to find you, with the amber marble I took from Harthacanute. But Canute and others have developed their skills to use a Time Tunnel. These tools are much more powerful and can take you anywhere. But in the hands of the corrupt, they can be deadly weapons. Normally you would have to stay within the boundaries of the tunnel, and your visit would be brief. But it is possible to step outside the tunnel if you have the knowledge. Canute must have passed this knowledge onto his son. There are dark forces at work. Time Regents can turn away from the services of good into the ways of the bad. Perhaps one such as this has influence in this quest. Perhaps we will never know how Canute came by his powers. It is possible that he was himself a Time Regent. Always be on your guard for Time Regents who have turned, Alice. Their tyranny is beyond compare. One day you may encounter one."

Alice twitched under a fleeting kiss of evil.

"Come on. We need to find Robert," she said.

"We will try together in the normal way. But if we are unsuccessful, all is not lost. I know one who can help us once we are back there," said Edwin mysteriously.

He took Alice's hand.

"Close your eyes and concentrate on finding Robert, Alice. Concentrate as you have never done before."

Alice took a big breath. She took her mind into a deep place that was still and quiet, floating in a space within herself. She called softly to Robert and began to see his face and hear his voice. She gripped the amber marbles tightly and let her breaths direct her thoughts. In seconds she felt her body lifting and the space around her and within her became one. It was bright and white and beautiful. Still she looked at Robert, deep into his clear blue eyes. With a thud, she landed on an earthen floor.

Alice had travelled once again, this time with a Saxon. She suspected that they had returned to the Manor of Newark not many years after the turn of the last millennium.

The ground was cool and damp. They were in a wooded glade. It was a clear night and Alice could see the swirls of distant galaxies peeping through the canopy of leaves above her.

She could hear the sound of voices. Edwin signalled to her to be quiet. They crept stealthily along the woody forest floor towards a red glow. Every now and again, Edwin glared at Alice when she stood on a twig.

"Sorry. I'm not used to this," she whispered.

"I can see that. These times are a lot quieter than yours. The twenty-first century is so noisy! You do not know the meaning of silence."

Alice was just about to retaliate with how foul the smells were in his time, when he pushed her down behind a bush. They peered through the shrubbery.

Men were huddled around a fire eating. The air was heavy with the odour of mead and horses.

"Is it Harthacanute?" whispered Alice.

"I can't see him," said Edwin. "Vikings did not ever settle in Newark. This is my grandmother's Manor. It is on the road used by the Vikings and they have many settlements around it, especially to the east, towards Lincoln. But Newark remains Anglo-Saxon. It gained its name from the *new work* done to fortify it with the ditch and mound around it."

"Actually, now that you come to mention it," said Alice. "I've never seen any Viking artifacts in Newark Museum. But I have seen lots of Saxon brooches and burial pots and things."

Edwin was watching the men carefully.

"These are mercenaries," he said. "Soldiers of fortune. Probably Danish. I wonder if Harthacanute has paid them to hide Robert?" Edwin started to look around.

Alice suddenly had an idea.

"We could text him," she said.

Edwin looked at her blankly.

"On his mobile phone," continued Alice. She took hers from the inside pocket of her blazer. "I can text him on this."

Edwin looked at the telephone warily.

"What does it do, this weapon?" he said.

Alice tried to keep a straight face.

"It's not a weapon. It's a way of talking to people who are far away."

Edwin's looked at her in astonishment.

"Show me how it works, then" he said.

Alice pressed the button to switch on her phone. But it was silent.

"Bother. Doesn't work. I suppose it needs a transmitter, and there aren't any in these days."

"So your little machine is no good?" said Edwin.

"No. Sorry."

"My eyes work though," said Edwin, bending down to examine some leaves. "This is blood."

Alice looked at him in alarm.

"Whose blood?"

"Look...there's more over here on this branch. It's low down. I think someone is wounded on the leg."

Alice shivered. She wished she'd had her school jumper on under her blazer. She looked down at herself. How strange she must look, in a Saxon forest in twenty-first century school uniform. There was a ladder in her navy blue tights.

"Come on," said Edwin. "There's a trail."

They crouched low and edged silently around the camp. Here and there, they found traces of blood on tree trunks and on the ground.

Some horses were tethered about fifty metres from the campfire. Alice trod on another twig and froze.

"Too drunk!" scoffed Edwin, looking at the men. He waved Alice on.

A few minutes later, they were level with the horses. Edwin patted a sandy coloured mare. She snorted affectionately at him.

"We might need these to escape," he whispered.

"But it's ages since I've done any riding," said Alice in alarm.

"And Robert?" said Edwin, looking surprised.

"Never," said Alice, shaking her head.

Edwin's eyes lifted to the heavens and he shook his head. "You will be punished if you ride your cars, and you do not ride on horses. How then do you get about?"

"Our mums and dads take us. Sometimes we walk

or use our bikes. There's always public buses and trains," said Alice.

Edwin shook his head again.

"Horses are easier," he said.

Behind the horses was a small clearing.

It was the edge of the wood and Alice could see distant ploughland and pasture in the moonlight. The coppice was being cleared here. Wood was stacked up ready for distribution to carpenters and craftsmen. In the corner of the clearing was a hut. There were no windows and the roughly made door was barred with a great trunk wedged into iron brackets.

"In there," whispered Edwin.

They edged round the clearing to the hut. Edwin walked behind it and stopped. There was a narrow gap between two of the roughly hewn planks that formed the walls.

"Rob!" whispered Alice. "Are you in there?"

"Yes," came a faint reply. "Get me out of here. My head and stomach hurt and my leg is bleeding."

14

Gallop at Sunrise

Edwin walked back round to the door.

"Help me with this log," he said to Alice.

Together they pushed and heaved. Suddenly it moved. Edwin caught the weight to prevent it from making any noise as it fell. He lowered it slowly to the floor and opened the door. It was almost pitch black inside and smelt foul.

"Over here," called Robert in a shaky voice.

"What's the matter?" said Alice. "Are you badly hurt?"

Her heart raced as she felt her way behind Edwin along the walls of the hut. Edwin stooped down. Alice's eyes were beginning to focus now. She could see Robert's silhouette slumped against the wall. Moonbeams splayed through the gaps in the walls like holy miracles.

"It's my leg," said Robert. "I tried to escape and they beat me up. I think my leg is broken."

"Try and stand," whispered Edwin. "I'll take your weight. Quickly. We must get you out of here. I will fetch some horses."

Robert hauled himself up, cursing under his breath at the pain. With Edwin and Alice on either side, they managed to drag Robert, hopping on his good foot, out of the shack. Edwin examined Robert's wounds in the moonlight.

"Umm. Not broken, I think. But quite serious. It was very wise of you to use your stripy neck rope as a tourniquet to slow the bleeding. I must take you to my grandmother. She will make you well. Wait here."

"Not sure our headmaster would approve of the use of a school tie!" said Robert.

"Bet he would. Probably give you some merit points for intelligence," said Alice, trying to sound cheerful.

Robert's leg wound was still oozing.

"Trust you to try and escape!" said Alice.

"Couldn't you just use the Time Triggers and get me back to the twenty-first century?" said Robert. "I think I might prefer a modern hospital to whatever our friend's granny might do."

"Impossible," said Edwin, returning with two horses. "The time travel would kill you."

Robert shifted miserably against the rough wooden wall. Alice smiled weakly. She tried not to cry.

"My *granny* is no ordinary woman, my friend. She will be able to mend you, do not fear. Come. Let us help you onto this horse. I will ride behind you. Alice, you must ride alone, though. I know you can do it."

Alice looked at the sandy mare in terror. She had once been fairly confident to canter through Sherwood Forest on pony treks with the riding school. But that was several years ago. And this saddle was a giant and the stirrups were far too long. She glanced back at Robert. Agony was written across his face as he shuffled towards the other horse. Her plight was nothing like his suffering. She steadied Robert as he reached up for the pommel on the saddle.

"I'll push," said Edwin. "You need to hold Robert's weight. Robert, you've got to pull yourself up, even though it hurts. Ready?"

Robert gulped then nodded.

"Go!" said Edwin.

Robert screamed. Bravely he kept on pulling and

Edwin shouldered his injured body up to the height of the horse. Robert lifted his leg and screamed again as Edwin and Alice shoved him into the saddle. Alice heard angry shouts from the camp.

"Go! Now!" yelled Edwin, mounting the horse behind Robert's slumping frame. "I have scattered all their horses."

Alice lunged towards the mare and used all her strength and gymnastics training to pull herself into the high saddle. Luckily, the leather straps above the stirrups had a loop just at the height for Alice's feet. She pushed her black school shoes through, grabbed the reins and a handful of the sandy mane and dug in her heels.

"Go, Sandy!" she yelled. "Ride for England! But don't throw me off!"

Alice galloped after Edwin. She had only galloped once or twice before. She talked to herself and the horse and tried to relax her legs. The rough edges of the saddle were cutting into her skin, but she did not slow down. Edwin led them through some more scrub land. They passed a charcoal pit and the last few trees before they sped into the empty countryside beyond.

The sun was rising. The horses followed a track behind some more trees and then down into a dip close to a village. Behind thatched roofs was a wooden church. Alice heard a cockerel crow.

They rode on. Alice was beginning to feel bruised in lots of places, but she clung to the horse's mane. Edwin seemed to know where he was going. They entered the cover of another wood and the horses slowed to a trot. They rode on, safe from any followers, but still Edwin did not stop. Every now and again, Alice heard Robert groaning as they jumped over a log or small stream.

At last they slowed. They were on a track between an avenue of trees. There was a large manor house ahead. Edwin walked his horse around to a paddock at the back and slid from the saddle leaving Robert slumped forwards over the neck of the sweaty animal.

A man rushed from the doorway. Edwin seemed to know him, and to Alice's relief, he seemed friendly. He could see them so he was probably a fellow traveller. She swung one leg over the back of the saddle and jumped down, panting furiously and wincing in pain. Edwin and the other man lifted Robert from the horse and carried him into the house. Alice followed them.

It was warm in the kitchen. A fire blazed in the range. Edwin swept some wooden bowls and vegetables from the table and laid Robert down.

"Fetch the Lady Godiva!" he commanded to the other man. "Here, Robert. Drink."

He poured a fragrant liquid into Robert's mouth from a leather pouch. Robert choked slightly and groaned. His teeth chattered.

"Robert!" called Alice softly. "Rob, can you hear me? Rob, don't go to sleep."

Alice looked up at Edwin. Fear gnawed at her.

"It will be all right, Alice," said Edwin. "Wait and see."

Just then, a woman swept into the room. She was young and beautiful. Her long, dark hair fell in unbrushed ringlets over her shoulders. She was fastening a robe over her night clothes, having just been woken.

"Edwin!" she said.

She embraced the young Saxon. She turned to Alice and smiled warmly at her.

"I was expecting you, my child," she said.

"But...you are so young," said Alice. "Edwin said you are his grandmother?"

The young woman laughed. She walked over towards Robert.

"And so I am," she said. "Or rather will be! His own father is not yet conceived."

Alice frowned.

"I am not quite in my own time, Alice," said Edwin.

"Ah! Yes, I see," said Alice.

Edwin had time travelled backwards too.

"My grandmother is a Time Regent. She prepared me for this when I was a small boy," he said.

15

Lady Godiva's Medicine

Lady Godiva bent close to Robert. Her smile had vanished. She looked very concerned. She gently pressed on his stomach and under his ribs. He groaned slightly. Then she opened his droopy eyelids and examined his eyes, before pressing gently over his skull. She tore back his trouser leg to reveal the large gash and loosened the tie slightly. A little fresh blood trickled out.

"He is gravely wounded, my friends," she said. "He has internal bleeding in his abdomen, probably from his spleen, and this leg wound has severed an artery. He has lost a lot of blood. At least his head injury is not major."

Alice staggered. She felt very woozy. Edwin caught her and helped her to a high-backed wooden seat. She burst into tears.

"He's going to die," she sobbed.

Edwin took her hand.

"No, he is not," he said.

He walked across to Lady Godiva and gave her his Time Trigger.

"What you are about to witness is one of the most powerful secrets of the Time Regents," said Godiva. "You must never reveal its happening to another."

Alice nodded meekly, wiping tears from her dirty face.

"A Time Regent can use the power of a Time Trigger to create a Time Tunnel and to hold it over an injured traveller to create a field of time change that will speed healing to almost an instant. This way, the traveller will not be further harmed by their wounds."

Godiva closed her eyes. She raised the amber marble and just as Cedric had done with the shell, she drew an invisible arch above Robert's body, chanting as she moved. A cold breeze brushed Alice's cheeks. She felt her stomach rise as if she was riding on a roller coaster and then a cloud of warmth floated across from the table. A tunnel of crystals slowly appeared from nowhere. It circled Robert and Godiva and seemed to pass right through the floor, table and roof of the Saxon dwelling. Still Godiva chanted.

As Alice watched, she saw Robert shudder, tense and then relax. He was quite still. Godiva's hands danced over him in graceful circles. Alice was silent. Edwin and the manservant stood motionless, watching. Then Godiva stopped her chant. She opened her eyes and looked at Robert. She touched the Time Trigger on his stomach and on his leg. Robert's eyes flickered and the tunnel vanished.

Godiva flopped forwards against the table. The manservant led her to another chair. She waved him away.

"It's all right, Carl," said Godiva. "I will be fine. Attend to our young patient. He will need to sleep now."

"Yes, my Lady," said the manservant.

He did not look surprised by any of this. Alice suspected that he had seen many strange things during his service in the household of a Time Regent. He carried Robert, who was now sleeping, through a doorway and put him gently on a couch close to the fire in the next room. He covered him with an embroidered blanket.

Edwin drew up a chair and poured three cups of wine.

He gave one each to Alice and Godiva and sat down with them, rubbing his dirty hands by the fire. For the first time in a while, Alice saw that he was grinning.

"A toast to Robert!" he said.

They all drank the warming liquor.

"Thank you," said Alice.

Godiva smiled.

"I have seen this day coming for many years," she said. "The dark spirits in Canute and others try to deflect you from your task."

"We still have to give the marbles, all four marbles, to the rightful king, don't we," said Alice, sighing deeply. "I don't even know who that is."

"Harthacanute will make it easier for you," said Godiva mysteriously.

"How?" said Alice.

"He will not find you here, though he will try. This house is well protected. This was his one chance and together with Edwin, you have foiled him. On his deathbed, he will give his Time Trigger to Edward, his half brother. Their mother was Emma but Edward is not Canute's child. The spirits have directed me and shown me that Edward is, at the moment, the rightful heir. I feel that there may yet be more to this quest, for I sense a darkness lurking. But for now, you and Edwin must return the other three marbles to Edward. I do not think that will be too difficult. I will aid you by bringing Edward here to this manor. He is a close friend of my husband, Earl Leofric."

"Now?" said Alice. "Without Robert?"

"Today. But rest awhile. Robert is still too weak to Time Travel. He needs more strength to make that journey. The two of you must go on alone."

Alice looked across at Edwin. He was dozing in his chair, exhausted by the night's adventures. His dirty blond hair and tunic were streaked with Robert's blood. His sleeping mouth was drawn into a contented smile.

Alice got up and walked through to Robert. He was sleeping peacefully. The two boys looked very similar in the firelight. Alice lay down on the rug beside Robert's couch. She felt herself drifting into sleep too, as someone covered her with a blanket.

She awoke with a start to find Edwin gently shaking her.

"Time to go, my friend," he said.

He pulled her to her feet.

"Can I suggest that you exchange your clothes for something warmer?" he said.

She saw that fresh clothing was laid out on the mat beside her.

"Where?" she asked.

"In there," said Edwin, pointing to a bedchamber beyond a curtained partition.

Alice examined her new clothes in the privacy of the bedchamber. She decided to leave her school skirt and shirt on, but she discarded her torn blazer. As she removed it, the left sleeve fell off completely.

"I'm gonna have problems explaining what happened to that," she muttered to herself.

She put a long-sleeved woollen tunic over her head and fastened it with a pale sash. She transferred the contents of her blazer pockets, especially her bus pass, into her skirt pockets. Then she wrapped herself in the soft, grey cloak and fastened it with the engraved brooch that had been left beside it. She stood up and smoothed the layers down around her ankles. She was much warmer now.

"Ah, ha!" said Edwin as she returned to the

kitchen. "A true Saxon Lady!"

Alice felt herself blushing slightly.

"A little food, Alice?" said Godiva.

"Yes. Please."

Alice was surprised at how tasty the flat bread was. And the stew was delicious.

"Lady Godiva, can I ask you something?" said Alice.

"Of course," said Godiva.

"Have you ridden through a town, well... without any clothes on?" said Alice.

Edwin spluttered slightly on his wine. Godiva smiled.

"You want to know if your myths and legends are correct about me?"

Alice nodded.

"Yes, they are. It was in Coventry last year. Earl Leofric is a pious man and a good man, but he sometimes gets a bit carried away doing his duty for the king. He was taxing the people so heavily, even on horse manure. They had to work so hard that they had no time for relaxing. They played no sport and knew nothing of the beauty of art. He said to me that if I rode through the streets unclothed in broad daylight, and that the beauty of God's creation was so revealed, that he would cease taxing them. Ha! You should have seen his face when I did it!"

"Did he keep his side of the bargain?" said Alice.

"Yes, he did. The people of Coventry were spared his tolls."

Edwin pushed back his chair.

"Come, Alice. It is time. We must time travel forwards from here to the early years of Edward's reign."

"Edward the Confessor?" said Alice.

"Yes, he will be known as that, for he is a devout

Christian who is often found in prayer," said Godiva.

"And you said he was Harthacanute's half brother?" said Alice.

"Yes," said Edwin. "Edward's mother is Queen Emma too. But remember that before Canute, she was the wife of the Saxon King, Ethelred. Edward is his son. Canute banished Edward to Normandy to get him out of the way and married Emma. But Canute was only recognised as king by Rome after he became a Christian. There are many who look across the channel to the Normans for support. And the Normans look back. Emma's family think they have a rightful claim on the throne of England. Like I said before, so many sons and so many pretenders!"

"Edward is the true king now," said Godiva. "He will soon have the fourth marble from Harthacanute. You must take the others to him for the prophecy to be fulfilled."

"Cedric said that Robert and I had a part to play in the outcome of the Battle of Hastings," said Alice. "Is this it? Will giving the marbles to Edward do the trick?"

"I am not yet sure," said Godiva. "After you have gone, I will consult the spirits. It may yet be revealed to me. And this Cedric...who is he?"

"He is a Time Regent like you," said Alice. "He guided us here. He is living in the twenty-first century. My nan plays cards with Mr Godwineson."

Lady Godiva and Edwin both looked at Alice strangely.

"Is that this Cedric's name...Mr Godwineson?" said Edwin.

"Yes. Why?"

"I hope it is just chance that he calls himself that

name. Earl Godwine is a treacherous man who will change sides to suit his own ends. There has long been a feud between Leofric and Godwine. I will consult the spirits about this," said Godiva. "Be very wary of this Cedric, Alice, if you encounter him again. There could yet be threats to the success of your quest."

Alice frowned and nodded.

"Can I see Robert for a minute, before we go?" she said.

The others nodded. She walked over to him. His face looked better now. He was smiling slightly. She could see that the wound had vanished from his leg.

"When will he be awake?" she asked Godiva.

"Soon. Go now. When you return the marbles to Edward, the power of the Time Triggers will take you back to your own time."

"What about Robert?" said Alice suddenly.

"Don't worry. When he is strong, I will return him to your time. There are ways."

Alice hesitated. She wished Robert had been well enough to go with her. But she trusted this Time Regent. Lady Godiva had healed Robert. Alice knew that she would continue to look after him.

"I'm ready," she said.

16

Tunnel of Evil

Edwin took her hand and they held their Time Triggers out in front of them.

"Farewell, young travellers," said Godiva. "Take care, always. The Confessor is a good man. But there may still be darker souls in this quest who seek to divert you."

Edwin gripped Alice's hand and she closed her eyes. She tried to concentrate her thoughts on the quest and meeting Edward the Confessor. Nausea rose within her and the whirl of time travel sent a spiral of colour through her thoughts. Her long hair, now loosened from its bobble, flamed behind her in the dust of galaxies that drifted past. In a dozen heart beats, she landed. Her time travelling powers had once again propelled her through the highways of time.

Edwin grinned at her.

"The power feels good, doesn't it?" he said.

Alice nodded. She looked around.

"Where are we? *When* are we?" she said.

"Looks like my grandfather's manor house," said Edwin. "It is not well kept now though. It looks like they don't come to stay at Newark much. My grandmother was thinking of giving Newark as a present to a monastery near Lincoln when I last saw her in my own time. She was always very fond of this manor. She will look after it."

"It's amazing to think of all the generations of people who have walked here, and will do after I, too, am gone," said Alice. "Simple folk, as well as

kings and queens. Families who eat and chat together, just as we do. People who have toothache
just like me. They have all the other struggles, like
getting about in bad weather or sleeping at night
when there's a storm. And then they are gone. If
they're not important, there is no record of them.
But they were here. They were real."

"You are right," said Edwin. "Your history books
are very detailed about the Romans. Not so much is
recorded of life during the five hundred years after
that. Yet so many lived. We Anglo-Saxons are skil-
led in art, more so than the Normans, from what my
grandmother tells me, but little has survived up to
your time. If the Normans do invade, they will not
usurp our language either, for your words are very
close to mine."

"I want to be an archaeologist," said Alice. Edwin
looked at her blankly. "Someone who investigates
the past. I want to put the clues together and try to
understand what came before. We are all here because of what has come before."

"I think you will be very successful, Alice of
Mercia," said Edwin, smiling.

"I suppose I do have a bit of a head start," said
Alice, looking around her. "School history trips are
a bit tame compared with time travel!"

"Come on," said Edwin. "We have a quest. Let's
take a look outside. My grandmother said she would
bring Edward here to us. We need to have a look
around."

Alice wrapped her cloak around her and they
wandered out into the overgrown courtyard,
avoiding some adventurous chickens. They walked
down the track between the avenue of trees.

"I can hear water," said Alice.

"That's the River Trent," said Edwin. "It's not far

across that field, beyond where that ploughman guides his oxen."

"Then my house will be built quite close to here one day," said Alice with a chuckle.

They reached the edge of a small village.

"Are we invisible?" said Alice.

"I should think so," said Edwin.

"What about to Edward?" said Alice.

"I think he will not be able to see us either. My grandmother said he was not a time traveller. The runestones said that the true king will not be."

"So how do we give the marbles to him?"

"I think he will be able to see *them*," said Edwin. "Let's try the church. There are horses over there."

The primitive church was built from wood, like the houses. An engraved stone cross, ten feet tall, stood in front of the door.

"How beautiful," said Alice, running her hand over its finally chiselled patterns.

They crept inside. The mud floor was strewn with rush matting. There were only two small, high windows, and they had wattle shutters. The room was lit by dozens of candles.

Alice saw three figures at the front of the church. One of them stood up and started to walk towards her. It was the Lady Godiva. She was older, but still beautiful.

"Well done," she said. "Earl Leofric and Edward are talking and praying. Things go well in the kingdom. I knew Edward would be a wise ruler. It is a good time for our destinies to merge to fulfill the prophecy of the runestones."

"Did Robert get back to the twenty-first century O.K?" asked Alice.

"Yes, he did. You will find him in your school playground where you left him," said Godiva.

"Thank you," said Alice.

"Follow me and do as I say. It is time. Leofric and Edward are not travellers so they cannot see you. But we must still take care."

Alice and Edwin followed Godiva. She signalled for them to stand in front of the king. His hands were resting on the back of an engraved chest with silver locks. Alice thought it looked familiar. Where had she seen a similar chest before? The king's eyes were closed. Something twinkled in the palm of one of his hands. Alice took a quick breath a she recognised the fourth marble.

"Take this, Alice," said Edwin.

He put his Time Trigger into her hand with the other two marbles. Alice hesitated. At the end of previous quests, Time Triggers had given her enough power to return to her own time when she touched them against something. There was very little furniture in the church, and no ornaments. But there was the chest. Perhaps she could use that. It would be easy to touch it as she replaced the triggers.

Holding her breath, she leant forwards. She gently brushed one of the marbles against the chest and held the Time Triggers over the king's hand. She glanced up at Edwin and Godiva.

"Goodbye," she whispered.

To her surprise, an icy blast billowed through the church extinguishing the candles. The doors flew open and a spiral of light filled the church, sweeping towards them like a giant torch beam. The force pushed Godiva and Edwin to the floor. The silver twister tracked round and started to advance towards Alice.

Alice fell forwards and for a moment, her hand touched Edward's. She felt a burning heat from the marbles between them as he grasped her. He looked directly into her eyes and screamed, before falling back into Leofric's arms.

"A beautious child! A spirit!" called Edward.

Alice was frozen with fear. She clenched her hands over the Time Triggers. Edwin struggled to his feet and drew his sword. It was too late.

17

Detention

The shimmering beam enveloped Alice and sucked her breath. Inside the tube, a face emerged through the vapours. Anger ravaged the friendly features she once knew.

"Alice!" purred the voice. "Let go of the Triggers, Alice!"

A mighty pain struck her upper body, shocking her like a current of electricity.

"No!" she managed to shout. "They are not yours to have, Cedric!"

She squeezed the marbles and closed her eyes. She needed to escape. She summoned the power of the Spirits of Time and thought of home. A powerful energy cut in, battling with her images of a Newark playground and trying to distort her vision.

"I will not give in!" she breathed, gritting her teeth.

The spasm of pain wracked through her once again, but it was not as strong this time. She knew she was winning. Harder and harder she forced herself to see the red brick school buildings. In a last breath of determination, she fell to the ground. The fury of the Time Tunnel vanished. Slowly she opened her eyes.

For several minutes, she did not move. Her breaths became less laboured and her pulse rate slowed.

"Are you all right?" said a lady's voice. "Did you fall? Are you injured?"

"I'm fine," said Alice, sitting up. She stood up shakily.

"You don't look fine," said the lady. "Come inside

for a drink."

Alice glanced around her. She was in the busy park beside Newark Library. It was the annual Water Festival on the River Trent this weekend and the town was bustling with tourists and stall-holders.

"I'm fine," said Alice. "I tripped on this long skirt."

The lady from the library looked at her suspiciously.

"You're very dirty. Why are you wearing this costume?" she said.

"Er...it's for the school. We're doing a historical float for the festival parade tomorrow. I was asked to nip out and get something for one of the teachers. I was in a hurry. I'm fine. I'd better get back."

"It's a very good costume," said the librarian. "But you do look as of someone has attacked you!"

"Ha!" said Alice.

The lady looked at her strangely.

"Thanks for your concern," said Alice.

Alice laughed all the way across the park. When she got to the public toilets, she went inside. She took off the cloak and tunic and rolled them up into a bundle. She did her best to smooth her hair and uniform and she washed her face and hands. Then she crossed the road and walked back to school.

The bell was ringing for the next lesson and the students drifted back from the playground. Alice looked around for Robert. She started to panic. What if Lady Godiva had been lying? Where was he? He could be marooned back in the Dark Ages. Then she saw him.

He was leaning against one of the gateposts, waiting for her to see him. He beckoned to her.

Alice threw her arms around Robert's neck and

hugged him. Then she felt a bolt of embarrassment and pulled away. But the look in Robert's eyes was soft and friendly. There was no trace of sarcasm. He looked as relieved as Alice felt.

"You took your time," he said.

She punched him.

"Have you any idea what I've been up to?" she said.

"More or less. Lady Godiva explained a lot of it. I know that I nearly died. Believe me, it felt like I nearly died!"

Alice smiled as she glimpsed the Robert she knew.

"But you don't know what happened with King Edward, do you?" said Alice.

"You gave him the marbles?"

Alice slowly shook her head. She held out her clenched hand. It was cut and bruised, and one thousand-year-old dirt now graced her fingernails.

"Oh, no!" said Robert. "Don't tell me! Please don't tell me you've still got them?"

Alice slowly unfurled her fingers. The four amber marbles sparkled orange in the sunlight.

Robert glared at Alice. He drew his hands over his face in frustration.

"Then we haven't finished," he said. "I'm really not keen on going back."

They were interrupted by shouting.

"Alice Hemstock and Robert Davenport! Come back inside at once!" shouted Miss Walton, the French teacher. "Didn't you hear the bell?"

They sloped back inside under her watchful eyes.

"You both look dreadful. The state of your uniform is a disgrace to the school. Detention, both of you. See me in the languages room after school."

She minced off. Robert groaned.

"That's all we need," he said. "What lesson have

you got now?"

"History," said Alice. "So have you."

Robert spluttered a laugh.

"That's fitting, at least," he said.

"We've got to talk," said Alice. "Things have changed a bit. You don't know about Cedric."

"What about him?" said Robert.

But before Alice could say any more, one of the teachers walked past.

"Talk at dinner," hissed Alice. "It's important. Take two of these. I don't think they should all be together."

She pressed two of the Time Triggers into Robert's hand. He nodded and winked at her as he opened the classroom door and babbled an apology for being late.

Alice shuffled into her seat next to Sarah.

"Pwor! You smell," said Sarah under her breath. "Respect for the messy uniform though!"

"It's a long story," said Alice, taking out her history file.

"...you did well with the essay," said Mr Picket. "Well most of you. The majority of you worked out that if Harold's troops hadn't been so far away and so battle weary after the Battle of Stamford Bridge, he might have been more successful at the Battle of Hastings. There was another key reason why William was so successful. Any ideas?"

Alice was half listening. The lesson reminded her of something Cedric had said. She and Robert were supposed to have a role in deciding the outcome of the Battle of Hastings. "Better not put my hand up and give that as a reason," she thought to herself, smiling slightly. She couldn't really believe anything Cedric had said now. Seeing his face in the murky Time Tunnel had been really scary. He was a

Time Regent who was now working against the quest. One of the truly dark forces Edwin had warned them about. He could obviously muster up some kind of power to create a Time Tunnel even without a Time Trigger. But then so could Godiva. Presumably that's how she had got Robert back. So what would Cedric's next move be? He wanted the amber marbles. Alice suddenly felt very afraid.

18

Curry and Sandwiches

"Maybe I'll have something to do with Harold's defeat," whispered someone in Alice's ear.

Alice jumped round.

"You again!" she said.

"Pardon?" said Sarah.

Alice glanced at her friend.

"Umm...sorry! Thought I'd dropped my rubber again," she lied.

"Behind you?" whispered Sarah, peering at the empty floor at the back of their seats.

"Yeah. It sometimes pings up off my ruler."

Alice glared at Edwin. He grinned back and folded his arms in amusement.

"Pinged off your ruler?" said Sarah. "Pinged how? Show me."

"Can't," said Alice. "Special trick. I can't just perform it on demand you know."

Alice started scribbling in her exercise book, copying notes from the blackboard. Sarah frowned at her before settling back into her own seat.

"I'd like to see that trick too," said Edwin.

He walked round to the front of Alice's desk and started moving her stuff about.

"What's this thing for?" he said, fiddling with her pencil sharpener.

"Stop it!" hissed Alice, snatching back the sharpener and hurriedly shoving everything back into her pencil case.

Edwin pretended to cry in disappointment. Sarah stared at Alice again. Alice gave her friend a cheesy grin.

The Saxon strolled to the front of the class.

"We need to talk, my time travelling friends," he said in a loud voice that only two people could hear.

Robert jumped. He gaped at Edwin then turned to Alice with a questioning look. Alice was standing up. She walked over to Mr Picket.

"I don't feel very well," she said in a quiet voice.

"You'd better go and see Mrs Atkins in the office then," said Mr Picket.

Alice nodded meekly, picked up her bag and walked out of the classroom, leaving the door open behind her for Edwin.

"Oh, Sir," Alice heard Robert say. "I'm late for my clarinet lesson. Please may I be excused?"

"I suppose so. Any one else got any other pressing engagements?" said Mr Picket sarcastically. "No? Good! Let's get on with history, shall we."

Robert closed the classroom door behind him. He grinned at the other two.

"It'll be lunch time soon," said Alice.

"Ah, food!" said Edwin. "I am famished."

Alice and Robert looked at him.

"These are *school dinners*," said Robert.

"Food is food," said Edwin. "Lead the way."

"If you're sure!" said Robert, shrugging. He grinned at Alice and led them down the corridor towards the dining room.

"It smells ... good actually," said Edwin. "Not goat or boar, I'll wager."

"It's cheese sandwiches, sausages or curry today," said Alice, reading from the weekly menu on the dining room door. "Oh, but there is chocolate pudding. We'll get some if we line up now. We're first in the queue. We can get a bit extra for Edwin."

The bell went for dinner and Alice pushed the door

102

open to get a head start before the crush.

"You're early, today," said Mary the dinner lady.

Alice and Robert smiled and nodded.

"I'm really hungry, Mary," said Robert. "Can I have curry and sandwiches?" He gave the plump lady his most eloquent smile.

"Um. Well...as no-one's looking!" nodded Mary. "Handsome fella like you needs to keep his strength up!"

"Thanks!" said Robert.

He piled up his tray and collected some cutlery.

"Edwin, take a pudding," said Alice. "Quickly, before anyone comes through that door!"

Edwin copied the others and they headed for a corner table. He had to shuffle about to sit down without removing his sword.

"Do you want curry or sarnies?" said Robert.

Edwin studied his options.

"I think the meat dish, if you are happy with bread," he said.

"Are you sure?" said Alice. "Not everybody likes curry."

"Ah...yesss!" spluttered the tall Anglo-Saxon, after scooping up a big helping of curry in his pudding spoon with the help of a knife blade. "Very spicey! But...not bad. Indeed, I think I could get accustomed to your dining."

They ate for a few minutes. They were all hungry.

"Umm. This sweet brown fluff is amazing!" said Edwin, devouring the chocolate pudding in three mouthfuls. "I have never tasted the like. It is very different from honey."

He wiped his mouth with his cuff and gulped down his glass of water. The dining room was filling up with dozens of other children now.

"Now, my friends, we must talk urgently," he said.

"About Cedric?" said Alice. "He is a rogue Time Regent, isn't he?"

Robert stared at her. Alice explained how she had seen his face and felt his evil in the vapours of the roving Time Tunnel in the church. Robert shook his head in amazement.

"Was Cedric the name he gave you?" said Edwin, after Alice and Robert had described their meeting with the Time Regent in Essex.

"Yes," said Robert. "Mr Cedric Godwineson."

"Of course! Ha! Ha!" Edwin almost fell off his seat with laughter.

"What's so funny," said Robert.

"He uses part of his own name," said Edwin.

Alice and Robert stared at Edwin blankly.

"His real name is Tostig, my friends. Tostig, son of Godwine, and brother of Harold. Tostig Godwineson, an heir to the Earl of Wessex and one of the most dangerous men in England. He would dearly like to seize the throne."

"But Old Toastie died on the battlefield at Stamford Bridge," said Robert.

"Your history books contain that record of this time line. It is one possibility. No doubt Tostig, as a time traveller, discovered this could be his fate. Now he seeks to alter history and create another time line. If he can gain possession of all four marbles together, perhaps he will be able to change his destiny and the fate of many others too. For the present, he must be weakened, but it will not be long before he tries again. There is not much time. We must return to my grandmother. If we return now to my own time, early in the year 1066, it will be the end of the reign of the confessor and the race to succeed him will be on."

"But who is the rightful heir?" said Alice.

"My grandmother now knows, I am sure. We must speak with her. Let's go."

"How did you get back here, by the way," said Robert. "We've got all four Triggers."

"Godiva generated a Time Tunnel. The highest Regents know more than is imaginable. They are very close to the Spirits of Time and have intimate understanding of the laws that govern our very existence in this universe. To them, travel is always four-dimensional. They do not fear the secrets of other galaxies. Their powers are beyond human comprehension. Even ordinary travellers like us are humble scholars in their presence."

"So Cedric...or rather Tostig, will be difficult to beat," said Robert.

"Not if we think cleverly, my friends."

Edwin stood up, almost pushing the plastic table over with his heavy sword. He started walking towards the doors. Alice couldn't help herself smile at the spectacle of an Anglo-Saxon warrior in the school dining room.

"Is there anything we should take with us?" said Alice, skipping to keep up with Edwin as they walked across the playground.

"I have wondered that, myself," said Edwin. "For now, let us consult Godiva. We could always return here, if it was safer. Now, where are the marbles?"

Alice took out one of hers and Edwin put his arm around her. Alice wrinkled her nose at the smell of leather, curry and unwashed armpits. Robert took her other hand and they closed their eyes. Alice drew her thoughts into a net of power, seeing clearly the pious face of Lady Godiva. She felt herself enveloped in a stormy embrace as the three adventurers swept back in time once more, towards 1066.

19

1066

"It is the Earl!" someone shouted.

Alice opened her eyes. The scissoring sound of swords re-sheathed echoed through the forest.

"My Lord!" cried the soldiers. They bowed low to Edwin, Earl of Mercia.

"Earl?" said Robert.

Edwin winked at him.

"My horse!" he commanded.

"Oh, no! Not more horses!" said Alice.

"You are a fine horsewoman, Alice of Mercia," said Edwin.

"Hmm. Didn't feel fine!" said Alice.

"We can manage on one this time, I think," said Edwin.

"Your men can't see us anyway, can they?" said Robert.

"They could do, if you surrendered the amber marbles to me," said Edwin. "But I do not think you should. You are the guardians. So we must ride together, friends."

Alice gulped as a magnificent warhorse was led towards them. One of the men helped Edwin up.

"Here," said Edwin, offering Alice his hand. He shuffled back on the large saddle.

She stood on his boot and levered herself up in front of him, then leant back, lifting one leg over the horse's mane. Edwin offered Robert a hand and Robert heaved himself up behind the Saxon earl. Edwin wrapped his arms around Alice and walked the beautiful animal on.

"We are not being pursued today," he said. "And we have my trusted guards. I think we can afford to ride a little more leisurely."

"That's fine by me!" said Alice.

It was a long ride across the medieval countryside to the house where Lady Godiva was staying. Alice was glad she was in front of Edwin. It was warm there. Robert had his blazer but she was just in a school shirt. She knew that they had travelled back to twenty or more years after they had last been here. She wondered if her blazer was still lying around somewhere in rags. Her mum was going to be really cross that it was lost.

"You are the Earl of all Mercia now then," said Robert.

"Indeed. I am Lord of a rich and fertile swathe of England. My grandfather, Leofric, was a friend to both Canute and Edward who both paid him well. The house of Godwine in Wessex is still the other great power in this England. Godwine's daughter, Edith, is Edward's wife, and her brother Harold is now the Earl of Wessex. Another brother you already know."

"Tostig?" said Robert.

"Yes, Tostig. He was Earl of Northumbria until his own people banished him for murder and treachery. Now he hides with the Viking King of Norway. The Vikings think they still have a claim to the English throne. The King of Norway claims that it was promised by Canute. Tostig had lined himself up with these Vikings, last time I heard. He wants to kill his brother, Harold, and make a try for the throne. With the immense power of the marbles, he may just succeed. My grandmother thinks Tostig knows we are onto him. He has probably seen that I am bringing you here. He has devices that let him spy on other travellers."

"The Shell of Destiny," said Alice.

They were approaching a thatched house. Edwin helped Alice from the horse and Robert jumped down. They followed Edwin inside.

It was a grand room for a dwelling of the eleventh century. Embroidered hangings decorated the walls. A portrait of a Lady hung on the wall together with painted images of saints. The furniture was adorned with silver and gold crosses. This was the home of someone who was a devout Christian and also a rare patron of the arts.

"Welcome, once again, young friends," said Lady Godiva as she entered the room. "I am honoured that we meet again. For me, it has been many years. But not for you, I think."

Lady Godiva was now an old woman. She was still beautiful and moved with grace and energy, her waist-length curly hair flowing behind her.

"I have seen him in my dreams," said Godiva. "Earl Tostig will not rest until he has the amber marbles. He thinks it is his destiny to be crowned king."

"Is it?" said Robert.

"No," said Godiva. "His brother Harold is not the heir of which the spirits speak, either. Some do say that King Edward named Harold as his heir. They do not speak true. The runestones foretold that the line would change to one of Norman blood. They were found by Canute, whose line might have prevailed if he had not tried to manipulate the prophecy for his own gain. He and his heirs were cursed, as you know. The reign of Anglo-Saxons in this country is drawing to a close. The English will have new leaders. Kings and queens of England will from now be descended from one man. This man is a Norman, although he is a great great grandson of a Viking. He is the one who must receive the amber marbles from you. It is up to you both to fulfill the prophecy and make history run true. This man is William, Duke of Normandy."

Robert started to smile. Then he chuckled loudly.

"What's so funny, Rob?" said Alice.

"I was thinking about our queen, in our time. You know...Queen Elizabeth. She's descended from William the Conqueror. If what Lady Godiva says is true, well...the queen's a Viking!"

A huge grin cracked Robert's face in two. Alice laughed.

"So, friends," said Edwin. "You have to work out a plan to get these amber marbles to Duke William, and the quest will be over, despite what the Godwineson brothers would like to do about being king. When Harold snatches the crown, he will be a usurper."

Alice stopped smiling. Lady Godiva's face was grey with fear. She was looking past them. Alice turned slowly, almost knowing who she would see.

"Not so fast, fellow travellers," said Tostig Godwineson.

Robert and Edwin span around. Edwin drew his sword. In his Viking helmet, Tostig looked terrifying. Anger and greed now slunk through his features. There was little that Alice could recognise of the mystic in Cragg's Café, except the hands that clutched his weapons. She knew it was the same man. But this warrior was not in any mood to talk. The edge of his sword was stained dark brown. Tostig Godwineson would murder anyone who stood in his way.

In his other hand he held a dagger.

"Do not move a sinew of your muscles," he said.

"Do not reach for the Triggers, Alice, or I will throw this dagger into your heart."

20

Trains and Buses

"Tostig, there are greater powers at work than you or I," said Godiva calmly.

"Ha! I am greater than you, that is for sure!" Tostig laughed cruelly. "You have done your best to outwit me, Godiva. But your regency is weak and puny. You think you are on the side of good and right. But what is evil? There is no such thing as good and evil. Only power. I have that power."

"Have you looked within the Shell of Destiny for your own fate?" said Godiva.

Tostig hesitated.

"I can undo what is written," he said. "I can start again. The throne of this island is mine. From here, I shall reach out and conquer the whole world."

"And then what?" said Godiva. "You will be the loneliest man on earth. Will you reach out to other worlds?"

"Perhaps," said Tostig.

"For what? What is there of value in all this conquest? True power is not to be found that way."

"Bah! This is the talk of a witch who would seek to distract me. You shall not!" boomed Tostig.

He lunged forwards and released the dagger. It flew forwards like a bullet. Alice gasped but Godiva did not flinch. Instead of piercing the lady's flesh, the metal blade ricocheted off, repelled by an invisible force.

"His anger and his pride will be his death," muttered Godiva.

Robert pulled Alice backwards as Edwin's sword

crashed down against Tostig's blade. Tostig grunted as he lifted his sword to strike.

"Go. Now!" shouted Godiva.

Alice had already gripped one of the Time Triggers.

"But..." she pointed towards Edwin.

"Now!" said Godiva again. "I will defend him. Fulfill your destiny."

Alice felt Robert's arm around her. She closed her eyes and in a flash they were time travelling. The journey felt more grey than white. Dangerous energies once more tried to interfere with their escape. Alice let her shoulders drop and took a deep breath. When she opened her eyes again, she was back in the twenty-first century. This time they had returned to the middle of a crowded shopping centre.

"We're in Nottingham," said Robert. "We must have ridden through Sherwood Forest to get here!"

"We're going to need a bit of luck to be back at school in time for detention," said Alice. "We won't be missed until then. But if we miss that, we'll be up in front of the headmaster!"

"Have you got any money?" said Robert, pulling out some coins from his trouser pocket.

Alice felt in her pockets.

"Oh, no. I gave my purse to Harthacanute instead of the marbles."

"Well I've got two pounds seventy-five. Let's see if it's enough for the train back to Newark."

They made their way down the hill, through the crowds towards the station.

"Pity we can't stay," said Alice, looking ruefully into the colourful windows. " I never get the chance to come here to the shops. They've got some wicked looking shoes and stuff."

"Maybe they'll accept priceless amber marbles in exchange," said Robert, smirking.

Alice punched him on the arm.

"You could do with some better gear," said Alice, giving Robert a stare.

"Yeah, O.K. School uniform is compulsory," said Robert looking offended.

"The thousand year-old blazer dust is cool though," said Alice.

Robert frowned at her. They studied the timetable at the top of the platforms.

"Bit of luck," said Alice. "There's a train to Lincoln that stops at Newark in a few minutes. Come on. We can't miss it."

The conductor on the train was in a good mood.

"You're twenty-five pence short for two half fares to Newark." He studied their torn clothes and dirty faces. "It'll do. Just this once."

He pressed the buttons on his machine and gave them their tickets.

"Phew!" said Alice. "That was close."

She looked across to Robert. She wanted to start planning their next move, but Robert had fallen asleep. Alice let her mind wander. She felt angry for having trusted Cedric, or rather Tostig. She remembered his shack behind the lifeboat shed on the beach in Essex. Surely there must have been clues there to warn them.

She tried to visualise the room again. "Of course!" she muttered "The tapestry on the wall! It looked just like the pictures I've seen of the Bayeux Tapestry. I think it was a missing segment. A comet and some ghostly spies. Tostig knew that meant the death of a king. But which king? Probably Harold or Edward. Did he think it meant he would be the next king? I wonder if there really was a comet visible in 1066."

When they got back to Newark, Alice insisted on popping into the library on their way past.

"I just want to look something up," she said. "Over here, in the history section."

Robert amused himself on the computer while Alice found what she was looking for.

"Halley's comet was visible in April 1066," she told Robert.

"What of it?" he said.

"Harold was on the throne by then. Everyone thought it was a bad omen. So did Tostig. That's when he came to look for us and the marbles, I should think. He thought it meant he could have a crack at being king. Some time around then, he tried to land in Lincolnshire with the Norwegian Vikings, but Edwin and the soldiers of Mercia fought him back."

"So where do we come in?" said Robert, as they walked back over to the school.

"We haven't got rid of these marbles yet, so I reckon Tostig could still try for them," said Alice.

The bell was ringing for the end of school. Children started to flock from every doorway.

"Come, on," said Robert. "Detention calls!"

They made their way against the flow of pupils and into Miss Walton's classroom.

"Ah, ha!" said Miss Walton. "I want you two to write out the school rules twenty times. Pay particular attention to the ones about punctuality..." She glared at Alice. "...and tidiness."

"Miss Walton," said Alice. "I should be at netball practice. Miss Thompson will go mad. I missed the last one because of the school play rehearsals and we're training for the tournament."

"Then you had better explain to her where you

114

have been and why, AFTER you have finished."

Alice scowled very slightly and started writing. She saw Robert mouthing "nice try" at her.

Alice scribbled away as fast as she could. It was hard to keep teachers happy. The drama teacher was not at all sympathetic if the rehearsals clashed with netball practice, and the music teacher said she ought to be going to orchestra if she was serious about playing the violin.

When Miss Walton wasn't looking, Robert passed her a piece of paper. "Are you going to the Water Festival tonight?" was written on it.

Alice nodded back at Robert.

He passed her another bit of paper torn from his planner. It said: "Meet there. Stay apart for now. Safer."

Again, Alice nodded.

"Have you finished, Alice?" said Miss Walton looking up.

Alice had. She couldn't spell very well, but she could write very quickly when she had to.

"Hmm. I suppose this will do," said the French teacher. "In future, please come to school properly dressed and look after your uniform."

Alice nodded meekly. Miss Walton waved her off. Robert winked at her. She ran past the deserted classrooms, her footsteps echoing through the empty corridor. If she hurried, she might just catch the late bus, as long as the P.E. teacher didn't see her. She walked the long way round the outside of the buildings, away from the netball courts, just in case.

It was lonely at the bus stop and a cold wind made Alice shiver. A cat leapt from the wall behind. Alice jumped. There was nobody about. She rubbed her hands to keep warm and tried to think of what she was going to say to her mother about the missing blazer. At last, the bus came. It wasn't the usual bus driver. This creepy man scowled at Alice when she showed her bus pass. Alice looked around at the other passengers nervously. They were all occupied looking out of the window or reading a newspaper. All except one.

The man on the back seat had a beard. The rest of his face was hidden under a tracksuit hood. He got up and slid into the seat in front of Alice. He smelt unwashed and slightly of horses as he rested one arm on the back of his seat. Slowly, he twisted round. It was Tostig.

21

Boat Race

Alice swallowed hard. She controlled her breathing and tried not to panic. She was trapped on the bus.

"I suppose you want the Time Triggers?" she said casually.

"Of course," sneered Tostig.

"But I haven't got them all."

"I know that. But two will do. I shouldn't have waited before. I will take them as I find them now, instead of all at once."

"You can't use them," said Alice, rapidly trying to think of a way out of her predicament. "You are a Saxon. Only one of Norman blood can be king. The comet hails your death as well as your brother's. That's why you came for me and Rob. We are the ghostly visitors, aren't we?"

The mention of the comet brought a shadow of fear across Tostig's face.

"Maybe it's your death, you precocious little child!" he said.

Alice was getting cross. Her dread turned to confidence.

"It is 1066 in your world, isn't it?" she guessed.

Tostig's eyes narrowed. Alice knew she was onto something. She needed to provoke him further. She wanted to make him really angry.

"Earl Edwin has defeated you once already. Harold might forgive you though, if you change sides. If you swear allegiance to him and come crawling back."

Alice knew she had hit a raw nerve now. Tostig's

lips snarled like a dog's.

"But then again, cowards are not well treated by their own side are they?" she continued. "The Vikings would probably kill a traitor, I expect."

"What do you know of anything?" roared Tostig.

He turned and kicked the seat in front of him in rage. A woman further down the bus stared at him. Whatever magic Tostig had used to get to Alice, he was not invisible.

"Nothing, actually," said Alice, springing to her feet and pulling the alarm cable.

The bus screeched to a halt, throwing everybody forwards, except Alice, who had been expecting it. She let go of the handrail and leapt past Tostig towards the front of the bus.

"Help!" she screamed, jumping out onto the pavement.

"Oy! You with the hood!" shouted the bus driver. Tostig ran towards him. "What the . . ."

Tostig pushed the skinny driver back into his place with the force of his battle-strong arms and leapt after Alice. She ran over the bridge that straddled the River Trent and down into the park beyond.

The Water Festival fair ground was beginning to come alive. Early evening customers strolled between the doughnut stalls and dodgem cars. Workmen on scaffolding were putting the finishing touches to the fireworks for the finale on the castle walls.

Alice dodged through the crowd. She could hear the shouts behind her as Tostig threw people aside in pursuit. She was heading towards the river. There would be no way out. Suddenly, she saw the tent for some kind of puppet show. She ducked inside and grabbed her mobile phone from her bag.

She texted Robert as fast as she could.

HEZ CHASIN ME @ FAIR. HLP!

She waited in the darkness of the little tent, trying to breathe silently. She peeped cautiously through the gap. Tostig was only several metres away, looking around him in rage. He tore off the hoody and pushed his long hair behind him. Sweat glinted on the muscles of his warrior's arms. Hastily, Alice ducked back. Had he seen her? She peeped again. He'd gone the other way. She decided to make a break for it. She was trapped if she stayed where she was. She bounded off towards the river edge where the boat crews were practising for the final of the boat race. They were wearing fancy dress. Incredibly, the members of one of the teams were dressed as Vikings. Alice almost laughed at their crude, bright costumes and plastic helmets.

A spare costume lay on the grass. Without hesitating, Alice scooped it up and jumped behind the bushes. She put the tunic over her school uniform and shoved the helmet on. Her heart leapt as she saw Tostig walking down the path in her direction. He had drawn his sword now.

She fled down the steps to the boat and called to the crew.

"Wait for me!" she yelled almost throwing herself into the long rowing boat as it cast off from the riverbank.

"Do we know you?" said the girl at the front.

"I'm the reserve cox," panted Alice. "I thought I'd join you...for a practice..."

The burly crew of rowers from the local farmer's group carried on rowing, grunting their battle cry with every stroke and taking the boat out into the centre of the river. One or two of them frowned at Alice. She smiled hopefully at them. Then she heard the commotion on the riverbank. Everyone turned to look. Another man in costume was pulling rowers from the boat behind. Some fell into the water and swam to the shore, while others backed hastily away.

Tostig climbed into the modern craft and pushed it off with an oar. He started rowing towards the Viking race boat with strong, fast strokes. The thin girl at the front of Alice's boat screwed up her eyes at Alice.

"He's chasing you, isn't he?" she said accusingly.

"Uh, huh!" said Alice guiltily. "And he'll kill me if he catches me."

The girl cox looked back at Tostig, who was gaining on them, despite being outnumbered by their rowers.

"Row faster, guys!" she yelled at her crew of amateur Vikings. They were heading for the bridge over the river.

"Alice!"

Robert was leaning over the parapet, waving at her. Alice pointed frantically to her pursuer and ducked as the boat passed close to the side of an arch under the bridge. She heard a loud thud in the boat behind.

"Get the police!" shouted someone on the bridge.

As she looked behind her, she gasped. Robert had jumped into the boat with Tostig.

The second boat emerged from under the bridge bobbing and swaying dangerously close to the narrow boats moored on the riverbank. Robert picked up one of the oars and turned to face Tostig.

"Oh, no!" screamed Alice. "Robert will be butchered!"

Tostig raised his mighty sword to strike. Then

Alice saw another man in medieval costume perching on the side of the bridge. This man was an archer. His bow was raised.

"Edwin!" said Alice.

"Who?" said the thin girl, looking for this next villain. But she could not see Edwin. Alice saw the shimmering light of a Time Tunnel around him as he drew back his arrow.

Edwin let go. The arrow flew with speed and found its mark. To Alice and Robert's horror, Tostig staggered back, clutching his neck. He disappeared.

22

Saxons, Danes and Normans

The policewoman was very kind. She took Alice's statement about the man who had chased her from the bus. Alice's mum gave her a hug as they left the police station.

"They're still searching, you know," she said. "But they haven't found him yet."

"They won't," said Alice calmly.

"You're being very brave about all this, Alice," said her mother.

"I think Robert was the brave one, jumping into the boat like that," said Alice. "He could have been killed."

Alice knew that for the second time in one day, Robert was receiving medical care. This time he was in a hospital emergency department. He had twisted his ankle.

"Can we go and see if he's O.K?" said Alice.

"Mrs Davenport is with him now," said Mrs Hemstock. "It's not too serious. You can ring him later if you like but I think he'll be back at school tomorrow."

Alice would just have to wait. Somehow she felt safer now. A shadow had lifted from her. Tostig was dead. Time Regents were mortals. He couldn't get them now. That reminded Alice about the Time Triggers rattling in her pocket. And that reminded her about her blazer. Somehow her mother had assumed she'd lost it in the chase. Alice decided not to correct her.

"Mum," she said, when her mother came to tuck

her in that night. "Is Uncle Jim going on one of his beer buying trips across to France again?"

"Now that you mention it, I think he did say something about a trip next weekend," said Mrs Hemstock. "Why?"

"I thought so," said Alice. She gave her mum a big hug. "Could I go with him, do you think?"

"Oh, I don't know about that, Alice," said her mum, taking out a clean school shirt for the morning. "I wasn't planning on another drive to Essex for a while."

"It would really help my history project," pleaded Alice. "Maybe Robert could come too?"

"Umm. What are you up to?" said Mrs Hemstock. "I don't think you and Robert should be out of our sight."

"Please!" begged Alice.

"We'll see," said her mum. "Now, GO TO SLEEP!"

Alice smiled to herself as she rolled over and got cosy under her duvet.

The next day was raining, which was good, because at least netball would be cancelled. Alice felt the teachers were watching her more than usual today. Mr Picket kept asking her if she was all right and even Miss Walton smiled at her. Everybody seemed to have heard of the hooded man running after Alice and the boat chase. No-one knew where he'd gone. One minute he was in the boat with Robert, and then he had vanished. Some people said he didn't even make a splash when he'd fallen in. The newspaper was speculating that he'd swum ashore and disappeared in the crowds. Another rumour was that maybe they'd find a body washed up further down the River Trent.

Alice and Robert had their own theory.

"I've asked my mum about going with Uncle Jim

on his trip to France next weekend," said Alice. "I reckon she'll let us. We could travel back from there to meet William the Conqueror."

"Umm. Not sure my parents are gonna be so keen, after yesterday," said Robert. "My ankle's not too bad, though."

The Davenports and the Hemstocks seemed to be getting on quite well. The parents had struck up a friendship since the children were seeing so much of each other. To Alice and Robert's surprise, they were allowed to go to France on the day trip, as long as they stayed close to Uncle Jim. They were going to drive back down to Essex with Alice's mother next Friday night.

The days sped by. Alice drifted towards her destiny. They could get the amber marbles back to William in France, she was sure. It was a brilliant idea.

But she was wrong.

She couldn't sleep on Wednesday night. Thoughts oscillated around her brain unchecked. She remembered it was play rehearsal the next day after school and she got up to pack her new jeans and hoody to wear. Suddenly, she heard a tapping on the windowpane. It came again. Someone was throwing stones up.

"Rob?" she said, flinging up the sash and squinting into the darkness. "What are you doing there?"

"I think you'd better come down," said Robert.

He pointed behind him.

"Edwin!" whispered Alice. "Uh, oh! This means trouble, doesn't it. Just a minute. I'll be down."

Alice grabbed her hoody and a stripy scarf from the back of the door and shoved them on over her pyjamas. She picked up her trainers and tiptoed down the stairs. The house was dark and still. The rest of the family was asleep.

In the silver light of the street lamps that shone through the kitchen window, Alice ran her hand along the wall until she found the duck shaped key rack. Luckily, the back door keys were hanging where they should be. She lifted them down silently and opened the door.

The night air was cold under the clear sky. Alice put on her trainers and crept round to the front of the house.

"That's not yours, is it?" she said, pointing to the silhouette of a sports car behind Edwin with its engine running.

"It's my new horse," said Edwin with a grin. "I needed a bit of practice to steer it, but it's not that difficult."

"Where did you get it?" said Alice.

"Godiva told him where to look," said Robert. "It was in the yard of unclaimed stolen cars behind the police station. We've borrowed it for the night. Goes like a rocket!"

"What do you mean, Godiva told him?" said Alice.

"My grandmother used the Shell of Destiny to locate transport for us. She recovered the shell from Tostig's lair," said Edwin. Moonbeams sparkled on his chain mail tunic. "She had another visitor last night. It seems we underestimated Canute. He must have time travelled forward again to check on his plans and discovered that Edward has named Duke William as his Norman heir. Canute is not a happy man. He could yet undo us."

Somewhere, an owl hooted and Alice looked over her shoulder into the blackness. Bats and shadows danced in the lamplight.

"Will he come here?" she said, shivering.

Edwin nodded.

"That is why my grandmother has sent me to assist you one last time," he said. "We must reach William tonight. The vehicle was my idea. Your machines are faster than my horses! We must ride to Hastings and look for William there."

Alice gulped. Edwin slid into the low driver's seat and revved the engine. Robert opened the passenger door and flipped the seat forward. With a sweeping gesture, he signalled for Alice to climb aboard. It was cosy in the back seat of the *Porsche*.

"Edwin, are you visible to people of our time?" said Alice.

"Yes. I can be seen, now that I have stepped outside my Time Tunnel without a Trigger," said Edwin. "Do you think my battle dress will start a new fashion?"

"Um...no," said Alice, smiling.

The roads were deserted now, save for the odd nocturnal traveller. Edwin drove the powerful car along the highways of modern Mercia.

They stopped at an all night trucker's café for a welcome drink. The unshaven man behind the counter gave them several stares, especially Edwin. Alice wasn't sure whether his Saxon robes or her stripy pyjama bottoms looked more weird. Robert was the only one dressed normally, in jeans. They hugged their steaming mugs and Alice licked her fingers after the last mouthful of her sausage and egg bap.

"That was gorgeous," she said. "What happened to old Toastie, Edwin?"

"Tostig died a traitor on the battle field at Stamford," said Edwin.

His face fleetingly clouded with sorrow.

"I lost many friends in that battle," he said. "Many good men from Mercia died to rid these

126

shores of Vikings. I do not think the Norsemen will ever return though."

"Something tells me Tostig was found with an arrow in his neck?" said Robert.

"Correct," said Edwin. He stood up. "Come, my friends. We have tarried long enough. Onwards to battle!"

Robert raised one eyebrow then grinned at Alice. Alice frowned back. These Saxons, Danes and Normans were a violent bunch. She felt for her Time Triggers where she had put them in a pouch around her neck for safety. Their smooth shapes felt warm, despite the cold night air. Alice wondered if the marbles could sense they were close to their destiny. She felt better after her snack and her fears turned to excitement as they sped on through the night towards Hastings.

23

Return of a Dane

The smaller Sussex roads had more bends than the motorway around London. But Edwin did not slow down. Their mission was urgent now. The future of England was in their hands. Alice felt sick, but the sturdy car cornered the curves with ease. Robert was trying to navigate by torchlight.

"It's not far now," he said. "We should be able to see the lights of the town over the next hill."

"Then we will stop here," said Edwin. The car jerked to a halt. "William built his fort up here, where he could spy on the old London road from his watch tower."

They climbed out of the sports car. Alice was stiff. She warmed her hands on the hot engine.

"So we time travel back from here?" she asked.

Edwin nodded. Alice and Robert took out the four amber marbles. Alice thought how small and insignificant they looked in the moonlight and yet these tiny stones had caused so much unrest and inspired so much treachery in greedy souls. The quest was not yet over. The three time soldiers now stood poised on the hilltop, ready to travel back to meet the man who hoped to conquer all England. But he needed the amber marbles. Without them the prophecy would not come true and the time line would shatter.

"Hold hands, guys," said Robert cheerfully.

Alice linked hands with Edwin and Robert.

"We want to arrive here in the early days of October in 1066," said Edwin. "After William has landed here with his boats and invasion forces and made camp. But before the battle with Harold."

"Won't King Harold want you to help him against William?" said Robert.

"When I left my time to reach you here, my forces had stopped in Mercia to re-group after our losses at Stamford. Yes, I should be following Harold. But my duty to the quest comes first. What happens now could change history. As my king, I have always been loyal to Harold thus far. But now the work of a time traveller takes priority. There are greater powers than those of greedy mortals."

"Let's get on with it then," said Robert, closing his eyes and gripping Alice's hand tightly.

Alice clenched her fingers over her Time Triggers and began to think of times gone by. She pictured a wooden fort above the town of Hastings and began to hear the shouts of men and thud of building work. The smells grew stronger too, of manure and leather and the molten metal of a blacksmith. They bathed her nostrils as the bright light turned and swirled around her.

They had arrived. It was approaching dawn on a misty autumn morning in the sixty-sixth year after the turn of the first millennium.

They were surrounded. The pointed tips of Norman swords engulfed Edwin. Alice and Robert, still invisible, were caught too.

"Oops," said Robert under his breath.

"Give me the Triggers," said Edwin. "Quickly! The Normans can only see me. They must be able to see you too. I am in my own time and will remain visible even with the Triggers."

Robert glanced at Alice. She took a deep breath. After all this time, she was being asked to surrender the precious objects she guarded. But she trusted

Edwin. His green eyes glinted warmly. She nodded at Robert. In the instant that they let go of the marbles, Robert and Alice became visible to the knights that surrounded them.

For a moment, no one spoke. The Normans froze in astonishment. Edwin broke the silence.

"Take us to your Lord," he said. "We have news of Harold Godwineson. We come as friends."

"Let me pass," said a commanding voice.

The circle of soldiers melted to the side. Alice knew this was the King.

"Earl Edwin!" he said with a heavy French accent. There was a dangerous mockery in his voice. "Another Saxon come to swear allegiance? Your kinsman, Harold, has turned traitor to his oath. And so might you."

"The clan of Godwine are no kin of mine!" said Edwin. He spat on the ground. "The Earls of Mercia are men of their word."

"Ha! We shall see!" laughed William. His strong features and cold blue eyes flickered with hatred. "I am most curious to know, however, why a Saxon earl should walk into my camp with two . . ." He paused for a moment, studying Alice and Robert. ". . . two peasants!"

"These are no peasants, my lord," said Edwin. "They wield powers that can change your destiny. They are the millennium spies who bear the mighty marbles foretold by the ancient runestones."

Duke William's eyes widened. He dropped his arms in surprise and breathed sharply. For a brief moment, he looked uncertain. His piercing eyes narrowed and his lips pursed above his beard as he stared at them.

"Bring them!" he commanded, turning back towards the fortress.

Four of the knights escorted Alice, Robert and

Edwin into the Norman stronghold.

"Sit," commanded the Duke. "You may leave us," he added to the nervous guards. He put his own sword on the table. "Show me the treasures."

Edwin opened his hand. The orange marbles glowed intensely in the firelight.

"Do they burn?" asked William.

He seemed in awe of the Time Triggers.

"They are only warm to touch," said Edwin. "But do not underestimate their power." He placed the amber marbles on the table.

"I do not, Earl. Believe me. I have heard rumours of this happening. Some say it is myth and legend. But my Viking forefathers have born witness to the runes that tell of two ghostly travellers."

"You must take these marbles and keep them safe," said Edwin. "When you take them, our quest is over. You will be king."

"And what of Harold? He musters troops in London now?" said William.

"You will have to defeat him," said a woman's voice.

William jumped round and stared. Lady Godiva smiled graciously at the Duke. Her steady voice continued.

"With the prophecy complete, you will be victorious. In fear and panic, Harold will soon engage you, but his forces are weak, and the Mercian army is still many days from here."

"The Lady Godiva, I presume," said William. He bowed slightly. "I have heard stories from the English of your strength and beauty. The legend is the truth."

Godiva walked towards them, resplendent in a blue and gold embroidered cloak.

"I have come to ensure that the quest is finished,"

she said. "These two young people are brave warriors in the fight against evil. They must hand you the Time Triggers."

William nodded respectfully to Robert and Alice. Edwin grinned at them.

"Take the Triggers, my young friends," said Godiva.

Robert pushed back his chair and picked them up. He reached across to give two to Alice. Before she had a chance to take them, Alice was struck by a mighty gust that came from nowhere. She staggered to the ground with Edwin and William. Edwin's sword spun across the earth.

A spectral tunnel sparkled into view. It was the Time Tunnel of a Viking. Canute, King of the Saxons and the Danes thirty years before, stood in front of Alice and Robert for the second time. He looked directly at Lady Godiva with his axe poised. Robert was trapped between them. In his hand, the amber marbles glowed red like fire.

24

Battle

Lady Godiva grew in stature. It was a meeting of time travel giants. Robert swivelled round to face Canute.

"You children have done well, for novices," said Canute. "Apart from falling under Tostig's spell, that is. You so nearly led him to his quarry. If he had got the marbles, we would all be dead."

"That's rich, coming from you," said Robert. "You've wanted us to play your own little games all along."

"This is no game, young man. The future is in your hands, quite literally."

Edwin shuffled towards his sword. Canute glared at him and raised his axe higher.

"Keep still, Saxon!" shouted Canute. "One more move and I will release this axe. Your friend will die." He turned back to Robert. "Now give me the four marbles. Delivered to me from your hand at last, the prophecy will still run true when I return to my own time. I will change history."

"You will not," purred Godiva.

She raised her hand and Alice saw the white and pink tips of the Shell of Destiny. Godiva lifted it above her head and began to chant. Canute tried to move. His arms were frozen. His Time Tunnel was not shimmering now. The walls were dark and the inside was cloudy. Canute's muscles quivered. He was paralysed.

Robert lunged across to Alice and they rolled against the fortress wall in the dust next to William.

Edwin leapt towards his sword.

"Aaarghh!" grunted Canute in frustration.

Edwin drew back his arm ready to attack. The chain mail on his tunic quivered. William staggered to his feet. He looked shocked and bemused. He seemed to be able to see something of the Time Tunnel.

"No, Edwin!" shouted Godiva. "Swords will have no power here. It is for me to finish."

Edwin hesitated. The Saxon earl and the Norman duke watched with Alice and Robert as Lady Godiva chanted on, imprisoning King Canute inside his Time Tunnel tomb.

Canute's eyes glowed red. In his Viking helmet and cloak his silhouette cast a dragon's shadow on the wall behind.

Still Godiva chanted. Alice felt the hot, electric power between the two Time Regents searing through the air, their wills surging desperately to overcome the other. The floor quaked.

Godiva's chant crescendoed. With a bolt of thunder, the Time Tunnel exploded into nothing and was gone. Godiva collapsed onto the floor.

"Quick!" shouted Edwin, running over to her. "Robert, help me lift her onto that chair."

"What magic was that?" gasped William, pacing around the floor where the Time Tunnel had been.

Edwin shot Alice a warning look. She knew that William was not a time traveller.

"There are many who would usurp you, William," said Godiva, breathing deeply.

"I know that, my lady, but whatever ghost was inside that device was not of this earth," said William.

"He was, my lord," said Edwin. "But quite mad. A tyrant enchanted by the spirits. But my grandmother has defeated him."

"Your grandmother is a mighty friend, indeed," said William. "You shall retain your lands and title, my lady, when I am king."

"My job is done," sighed Godiva. "Alice and Robert must do theirs now."

"Did you...er...kill Canute?" asked Robert.

"No," said Godiva. "But he is banished from time travel. I sent him back where he belongs to his natural life, and death. A shame, really. I used to enjoy his roguish company at Regent's gatherings...until he grew greedy and tried to change destiny, that is."

"Did you meet Tostig?" said Alice.

Godiva's face darkened.

"Yes and I have always feared him," she said. "But now my heart is light. I can rest at last."

"So!" said Edwin. "All that remains is for Duke William to take those amber marbles, is it?"

William of Normandy smiled at the young travellers with his clever, ruthless eyes. Alice knew King Harold was riding here right now and bringing many of her ancestors towards their bloody death. William would show no mercy to those who opposed him. She took a deep breath. She was very tired.

"We need to get back home," she said.

"And you are far from where you live, I think," said Godiva.

"I could always drive the *Porsche* back," suggested Robert, grinning.

"I shall miss your time," said Edwin. "I enjoyed your metal chariots and your food."

"My men will let you pass and give you fresh horses," said William. "And you are welcome to share food and wine before you go."

"That's very generous of you, my...er...lord," said Robert, addressing the man who would be king. "But I think you're missing the point. Your horses cannot ever take us where we need to go."

William looked offended.

"I think I have the answer," said Godiva.

They all looked at her.

"The Shell of Destiny can work its magic one more time," she said.

Robert raised one eyebrow as she pushed her chair back.

"My Lord William," said Godiva. "There are mystic ways that you cannot understand. What you are about to see is not for the eyes of the unchosen. But since your destiny and this quest are interwoven, I see no choice but that you witness what must be done."

William bowed graciously.

"What should I do?" he said.

"Take us to where you arrived, Edwin," said Godiva.

William opened the door and they walked back towards the hilltop above Hastings. Alice heard the quiet clatter of men eating and resting in the moonlight. On one side of the hill, William's fleet lay moored in the watery bay of the English Channel. On the other side, she could just make out the London road snaking through the scarred moors and marshland and the gentle rise of English woodland beyond. Not many hours from now, this corner of England would be swarming with horses, archers and infantry locked in deadly combat.

25

Charms and Brooches

They reached the place where Edwin had parked the car in the twenty-first century.

"But how will we get back to Newark?" said Robert.

"When you place the Time Triggers in the Duke's hand you must hold the shell with the other and concentrate your thoughts on being in Newark," said Lady Godiva.

"But I thought we could only go back in time on the spot, not switch places, even with Time Tunnels," said Alice.

"Normally, that is the case," said Godiva. "But there are some Time Triggers that are very powerful and special. The Shell of Destiny is one of these. They can create a tunnel that will take you on a journey across the geography of the universe as well as through the highways of time. I think you are ready to make such a journey."

"Will it hurt?" said Robert.

"No, child," said Godiva, smiling. "Are you both ready?"

"I will miss you, my lady, and you too, Edwin," said Alice. "Oh, and you, too, William...my lord," she added hurriedly, with a curtsy.

"We may meet again," said Edwin.

"That would be good," said Robert. "Next time we'll have to take you to a football match."

Edwin looked at Robert blankly.

"Or the cinema...or shopping," said Alice. She tried not to laugh at the thought of a Saxon earl clanking through a supermarket.

"As long as I can ride one of your metal machines again," said Edwin, grinning. "That was ... er... cool!"

"That reminds me," said Robert. "We left the car miles from Newark. Oh, well, I suppose the police will find it eventually."

"Do we need to take an object from this age and touch it against the Time Triggers to give us the energy to get home as we have done before?" said Alice.

"Not this time," said Godiva. "The shell has more than enough energy to do the job."

Alice looked disappointed.

"But I would like you to keep this," said the Saxon lady, offering Alice an engraved silver brooch, inlaid with jet, glass and amber.

"Oh, thank you," said Alice. "It's more beautiful than anything I've seen in my time."

"And Robert should have a souvenir," said Edwin.

He took off one of the leather pendants that decorated his neck. It had a silver, cross-shaped charm. One way up it almost looked like the hammer of the Viking god Thor, but the other end was cast as a dragon's head.

"This was given to me by my grandfather. It will protect you from evil and bad luck," said Edwin.

"Wicked!" said Robert, examining the fine piece of ancient jewellery.

"You will need it," said the young Saxon. "I think you will make many more journeys as a time traveller."

"Cheers!" said Robert, nodding at Edwin.

William had been watching the road at the foot of the hill.

"We must hurry," he said. "The dawn is rising. I

must ready my men for battle."

"I, too, must depart," said Edwin. "I will take my grandmother to safety and return to my army. We shall not be joining Harold in this battle."

"I will remember you, Edwin of Mercia. My scouts tell me that your town of Nottingham would make an excellent base to build one of my new castles. Castles will be the way to govern the chaos of this island. I will build many."

"Then I shall see you in Nottingham," said Edwin. He turned to Alice and hugged her. "In another life we could have been great friends, even husband and wife," he said.

Alice heard a little snigger from Robert. She felt herself blushing.

"Thanks," she said to Edwin, laughing. "But I wouldn't like to spend my life galloping between damp castles."

"The history books do not do you justice, my Lady Godiva," said Robert, bowing.

"Save your flattery for younger women," laughed Lady Godiva. "Give Alice two of the amber marbles and place your other hand on the shell with hers. Good. Now give them to Duke William of Normandy and the prophecy of the runestones will at last be true. The bloodline of the kings and queens of England will from now descend from him. That is his destiny."

Alice and Robert touched the shell as William held out his hand. They placed the Time Triggers into his palm.

"Goodbye Alice and Robert of Mercia!" said Edwin.

Alice closed her eyes.

"Concentrate your thoughts on going home," called Godiva.

The voices and noises of the last millennium faded. A storm of colour raged in Alice's mind. She heard again the voice of Cedric Godwineson.

"There are ways of seeing," the voice said.

Alice looked and saw. She heard and smelt and felt as well. Her senses were flooded with immeasurable delicious stimuli from across the galaxies as she sped onwards through the swirls of time itself. She saw her house and the lamp-post outside her bedroom window. Then she heard the horn of a passing car and opened her eyes. They had arrived back in the middle of the street outside her house. It was dawn.

"Wow!" said Robert, sitting down on the little wall in front of Alice's house. "What a night!"

He was admiring his new pendant. "I'll always wear this under my shirt," he said.

"I'm going to be SO tired at school today," said Alice.

"At least you're alive. Think of the slaughter on the battlefield at Hastings after we left. The stench...the cries...the blood spouting..."

"Yes! O.K. O.K. I've got the point," said Alice. "Are you coming in for breakfast?"

"Better not. Your parents will think I'm your boyfriend or something!"

Alice rolled her eyes in horror.

"Well, I'll see you at school," she said.

"Wonder what we'll be doing next in history?" said Robert.

"I don't mind, as long as we don't find any more Time Triggers for a while. I need a rest."

"Hey! Don't forget we're off to France on a ferry at the weekend to buy some wine, with your uncle," said Robert. "I'm looking forward to meeting your nan again and taking Keeper for a walk."

"Me too. No more kings and Regents and Time Tunnels I hope!" said Alice. "Just bacon butties and games of cards. Mind you, Nan always likes to gamble when we play. That can be pretty scary!"

Alice jumped up and headed into her driveway. She needed breakfast. Her tummy was rumbling. The lack of sleep was making her feel sick.

Alice looked over her shoulder into the morning mist. She heard the distant clatter of metal. It was a strange sound and it was mixed with the roll of hoofs and shout of voices. It could almost be the sound of many men locked in battle.

The feeling passed. She opened the back door and crept up to her bedroom. They had triumphed. The quest was finished. This time.

MORE TITLES

IN

THE TIME TRIGGER SERIES

Alice and Robert live close to Newark Castle in Nottinghamshire, where there has been mysterious flooding, and where King John was murdered in the Middle Ages. On a school trip to France they team up with a French boy called Jean-Marc and embark on a treacherous quest to unlock some secrets of the past that will take them back to Ice Age caves and medieval castles. But time is running out.

A very flowing, well-written, imaginative story
Macmillan Children's Books

A really good read... an excellent tale... I was so into the story I didn't have time to watch the Simpsons!
Nicole (aged 10) in "CountyLit" Magazine

An intriguing idea... there is excitement and mystery which should appeal to young readers
Writers' Advice Centre for Children's Books

Dragonheart Publishing   ISBN 0 9543773 0 3   £5.99

THE KEYS OF
ROME

Robert and Alice arrive in Rome where the pizzas are fantastic. They discover mysterious and powerful Time Triggers with links to the English City of Lincoln. In this adventure, the two friends surf the waves of time once more and travel back to the murky underworld of Renaissance Italy, where fine art abounds but the gallows are never far away. Their quest will propel them even further back in time, to the cruel Rome of the Imperial Caesars. Alice and Robert must unravel the truth amongst the secrets and murder before it is too late.

A clever and intricate time-slip novel. This is an inventive drama... with entertaining historical insights, including an intriguing explanation as to why Caravaggio was such a ground-breaking artist.

Times Educational Supplement, Teacher Magazine

A tremendous ten out of ten!

Zoe (aged 10), Newark Advertiser

... highly entertaining new time travel novel aimed at young readers

Nottingham Evening Post

Dragonheart Publishing   ISBN 0 9543773 1 1   £5.99